Victorian Horror Stories

Retold by Mike Stocks
With introduction and notes by Anthony Marks

Illustrations by
Adrian Chesterman & Lee Stannard

First published in 2002 by Usborne Publishing Ltd,
Usborne House, 83-85 Saffron Hill, London
EC1N 8RT, England.
www.usborne.com

A catalogue record for this title is available from
the British Library

ISBN 07460 5123 9

Printed in Great Britain

Edited by Felicity Brooks & Anthony Marks
Designed by Brian Voakes
Series editors: Jane Chisholm & Rosie Dickins
Cover design by Amanda Gulliver

CONTENTS

About Victorian Horror Stories

The stories in this book have one very important thing in common: they were deliberately written to scare their readers. These days, if people want to be scared, they might go to see a horror film. But most of these stories were written in the second half of the nineteenth century, during the reign of Queen Victoria, before cinema as we know it had been invented. People in those days enjoyed the thrill of being shocked and frightened just as much as they do today. The public at that time had developed a huge appetite for macabre or gruesome subjects, and horror stories were frequently published in magazines and newspapers – both in Europe and America. Huge improvements in printing technology meant there were now far more of these to read. Improving educational standards meant that there were far more people to read them. In turn, this meant there were more writers – although it isn't always exactly clear, over a hundred years later, who wrote what.

We know the authors of some of the stories in this book. Two of them are American: Fitz-James O'Brien, who wrote "The Beast from Nowhere", and W. C. Morrow, the author of "An Original

Revenge". A British author, Samuel Savage, wrote "The Cat". But the other tales have more mysterious origins. They seem to be alternative versions of ideas − about werewolves, hauntings and grisly murders − that had been around in myth and legend for centuries. "Let Loose", one of the stories in this book, is based on two similar stories − one by a French writer Guy de Maupassant, the other by the British writer Mary Cholmondely. The roots of others are harder to trace. We know from the setting and the names of the characters that "The Head of Jean Cabet" is a French story, but we cannot track down the name of the person who wrote it. "One Silver Bullet" takes place in London's financial quarter and refers to several streets and alleys by name, implying that its author was very familiar with the city.

But, whatever their origins, all the stories are shocking. Like plenty of Victorian stories, they explore aspects of the supernatural. But these go further than most. They describe − often in detail − gory scenes of raw terror. Blood runs through them like a constant stream. Even the two stories that feel most like psychological thrillers have bloody endings. Ghost stories leave readers feeling uneasy; but these stories leave readers with lasting images of real horror.

Why did people at this time feel such a need to read this kind of story? There could be many reasons. The growth of science and technology in the nineteenth century encouraged many people to feel that knowledge and industry would eventually bring the world's problems to an end. Yet they continued to see sickness, poverty and war, either on their own doorsteps in the inner cities, or reported from abroad by newspapers and photographers. For most people, rich and poor alike, disease and death were never far away. Scientists were slowly discovering cures for fatal illnesses such as cholera, typhoid and tuberculosis, but huge numbers of people still died from them each year. In a way, people wanted horror stories to help them to come to terms with everyday life. If the stories were more shocking than anything people could see in the world around them, then somehow that world, frightening as it was, didn't seem quite so hostile.

These horror stories also question the powers of scientists and people with knowledge. In "The Beast from Nowhere", the scientist is the first person to meet his death. In "Let Loose", it is the quest to know more about the fresco in the church that unleashes the evil power. And because of knowledge he acquires in a library, the hero of "One Silver Bullet" is forced to make a terrible sacrifice. The constant presence of blood turns an object of scientific discovery (it is around this time that scientists were beginning to understand the purpose of blood and how it works) into a symbol of horror. In these stories, no matter how much they know, people are still forced to confront the unknown. And just as this fascinated the Victorians, it continues to fascinate us today.

Let Loose

People think I'm odd because I always wear an old-fashioned high collar. I know that they joke about it behind my back, and to my face they express amazement that I still wear one even on the hottest of summer days. In short, people are always wondering *why*. But I never tell them. I don't dare. If they knew what my collar concealed, they would be utterly horrified. If I took my collar off, they'd probably scream.

I'm an architect and an art critic. Ten years ago, I was asked to make a speech on a subject close to my heart: English frescoes. A fresco is a painting done on a wall, usually with a religious theme, and there are examples scattered all over England. Reading a book called *The English Fresco in the Northern Counties* in preparation for my talk, I came across a handwritten note scrawled at the bottom of a page: "Wetwaste, Yorkshire – truly exquisite example of early English fresco in church crypt." My curiosity aroused, I immediately decided to go to Wetwaste to have a look at this "exquisite" fresco.

The journey by train and mail coach was as tiring as I'd expected, and at the end of it there was a five mile trek across a wild moor to the remote settlement of Wetwaste itself. I was exhausted by the time I arrived, but Brin enjoyed the walk. Brin was my dog. He had the appearance, not to mention the teeth, of a wolf, but in fact he was as gentle as a kitten.

Wetwaste was the bleakest, most miserable spot you can imagine. Two straggling rows of grey cottages flanked the single mud road, which had a scruffy inn standing at one end, and a gloomy church at the other. Thoroughly worn out, I went into the inn and asked for a room. It wouldn't have surprised me if I was the first stranger to have passed through that village in many years, because my simple request provoked astonishment.

In the morning, while I ate my breakfast of bread and cheese, the innkeeper's family and half a dozen villagers watched me, as though I were an exotic beast from a faraway land. I remember in particular a little girl, who had a dirty face and bare feet, gaping at me in amazement. It was a relief to finish my breakfast and go to look for the local clergyman.

He lived behind the church, in a parsonage built from the same drab stone as everything else in the village. An ancient servant showed me into a small, book-lined study, where his equally ancient master was dozing in an armchair.

"Good heavens," he exclaimed, waking up as I was announced.

"Excuse me for disturbing you."

I introduced myself, and after the usual formalities explained that I hoped to look at the fresco in the crypt of the church.

"The crypt?" he repeated in disbelief. "It's been locked for nearly fifty years."

"Can you give me the key?"

He shook his head.

"Why not?"

He looked almost frightened as he slumped down in his chair.

"I'm afraid I can't tell you that. You wouldn't believe me if I did."

I have a reputation for always getting what I want. Glancing around the cluttered study, I looked for a way of getting the old man onto my side. I noticed that there were many books on birds.

"Do you get many peregrine falcons in these parts?" I asked.

"Yes! Magnificent birds, Mr., er, ah..."

"Blake."

"Does ornithology interest you, Mr. Blake?"

"Passionately," I lied.

His eyes lit up.

"Well sit down, make yourself comfortable. Perhaps you'd like a cup of tea?"

We talked – or luckily, he talked – about birds: flycatchers and finches, grebes and geese, warblers, waders and wagtails. Within half an hour he was slapping me on the back with delight and treating me as if I were an old friend. So I raised the subject of the crypt once more.

"Ah," he said with a long, melancholy sigh. "What you don't realize, Mr. Blake, is that the crypt frightens the villagers. You see, something happened a long time ago and they would be *appalled* if they knew the crypt had been opened again. The people here are very superstitious."

"Who needs to know except us?" I asked.

"Yes... Well, I'm not sure."

"The Church of England has always disapproved of superstition, hasn't it?" I asked innocently.

"Yes... Of course, I don't believe in these superstitions *myself...*"

"No man of your intelligence *could*," I murmured, hoping that flattery might work.

"Er, quite," he replied hesitantly.

He stood up and unlocked an oak cupboard in the corner, from which he extracted two keys. He paused, dangling them tantalizingly from his fingers, and then turned to me.

"I will give you these keys," he told me gravely, "but only on condition that you grant me one request."

"Of course."

"The crypt is at the bottom of a flight of steps outside the north wall of the church. There are two doors. This key opens the outer door, which lets you into a small passage. As soon as you get into the passage, you must lock the door behind you."

"All right."

"This slightly larger key opens the inner door, which leads to the crypt itself. You must enter the crypt quickly, shutting and locking the door behind you immediately. Do you understand?"

"Of course."

"When you leave the crypt you must follow the same procedure in reverse. Now – will you give me your word that you'll do as I say?"

"I give you my word."

"Very well. Try to forgive what must seem to you like an old man's nonsense, but if you knew what I know about the crypt..."

"What do you know?"

That was something that the old parson simply refused to divulge.

I nearly fell down the flight of steps when I explored the north wall of the church. Grass and weeds had grown over the entrance so thickly that it was entirely concealed. I glanced around to check that no one was watching, then pushed the grass aside and carefully climbed down the damp, mossy steps.

"Brin! Come here!"

With great reluctance, my dog followed me down. I lit a candle, and with my free hand I put the smaller key in the lock of the outer door. After some difficulty, I was able to turn it. Then I grasped the handle and pulled. I gradually increased the force until I felt the old door shift on its hinges. It was ready to open.

Because I had given my word to the parson, I felt there was no choice but to follow his meticulous instructions. I pulled the door open as quickly as I could, bundled Brin inside the small passage, stepped in myself, and slammed the door shut. It was particularly unpleasant in there, slimy and smelly, and Brin whined piteously as I locked the outer door. I quickly turned to the inner door and inserted the key in the lock. Soon we were both inside the crypt.

Before I did anything else I lit some more candles, until the whole interior was illuminated. We were in a low chamber, cut from solid stone, with rough archways and crude pillars supporting the roof. On one wall was an extremely grisly sight: hundreds of bones and dozens of skulls arranged on a stone shelf, all piled up on top of one another so that they almost reached the ceiling. But on the opposite wall was the most brilliant fresco I had ever seen.

It was quite miraculous that this beautifully accomplished painting existed in such a remote spot. The subject matter was the Ascension, the passing of Christ from Earth to heaven. I estimated that the fresco dated from the earliest part of the fifteenth century. The quality of its finish, and its near-perfect condition, made it unique. Almost trembling with excitement, I set up my easel, arranged my pencils, and began to sketch.

Though I was absorbed in my work, I noticed that Brin was finding it difficult to settle. There was nothing surprising in that; I could hardly expect him to share my own pleasure in frescoes. But after more than half an hour he still hadn't decided on a comfortable spot. I had to order him to lie down. He reluctantly obeyed me, and remained for the rest of the day under the low shelf of bones, watching me uneasily with his head on his paws.

It felt as though I'd been there barely an hour when, looking up, I noticed the candles had burned low. It was already six o'clock in the evening. I started to pack up my easel. Brin leaped to his feet and rushed to the inner door, pawing at it eagerly. He seemed to become more and more desperate to leave, until, by the time I was standing next to him at the door, he was butting it with his head and whining miserably.

I put the key in the lock and opened the door. Brin shot out into the little passage, so that I was briefly alone in the crypt. At that moment, something happened. I like to think I am not easily frightened, but I heard a noise behind me which made me jump out of my skin. It wasn't a quiet noise. It was a full-bodied *crash*, like the sound of a vase smashing on the floor. The hair on the back of my neck stood up, and an unpleasant tingling sensation went down my arms. I turned around slowly and, with just one lit candle in my hand, went back into the crypt.

On the floor, below the shelf of bones, was a skull. It was shattered into many pieces. After the initial shock of seeing it, I felt rather relieved. For over fifty years the crypt had remained untouched, so it was hardly surprising that my entry had disturbed things in some way. A movement of air had dislodged the skull from its precarious perch, perhaps. Who knows? I picked up the pieces – after all, what were they, but chunks of calcium phosphate? – and placed them carefully on top of the other bones and skulls. Then I went out into the passage where Brin, trembling, was waiting for me, and locked the door of the crypt behind me.

I have to admit to a feeling of particular uneasiness in the small passage. Perhaps it was Brin. For some reason he was terrified. The light of the candle was quite weak, not fully illuminating the floor or the corners. I fumbled with the key.

It was as I was pushing the outer door open that something brushed against my leg. At the same time, I thought I saw something shoot out of the door when a chink of a few inches appeared. It's hard to say what I saw. A rat, maybe? Could a rat survive in there? Whatever it was, it seemed to *scamper* out of the door. Then, as soon as the door was open wide enough, Brin charged out too, followed closely by me. It was good to feel the fresh air. I decided that I had seen a rat, and that if I wasn't careful I'd end up as foolish and superstitious as Parson Patrick Higgins himself, to whom I returned the keys.

The next morning I went down to breakfast and discovered that something tragic had occurred. The little girl with the dirty face and bare feet had died during the night. She was the daughter of the people next door, and the innkeeper's wife was in tears as she served me my breakfast. I asked her what the little girl had died of – the child had seemed healthy enough the previous day, if a little undernourished – but I found her broad dialect almost impossible to understand, and anyway she was crying too much. All I could find out was that the poor little girl had been found lying dead in the bed she shared with her sisters.

It was a tragedy, a tragedy that I mulled over often during the course of the day; and yet it didn't prevent me, after I had finished my breakfast, from collecting the keys and going back to the crypt so that I could continue with my sketch. I was a stranger in Wetwaste, and could offer nothing but my sympathy. It was better that I kept out of the way and left the family and their friends to help each other.

When the parson handed over the keys, he made the same cautious warnings that he had delivered the first time. He obviously wasn't aware that there had been a death in the village, so I told him about it. He immediately called for his coat, and set out to minister to his stricken parishioners.

It was an uneventful day in the crypt. I left Brin outside to chase rabbits, as nothing would induce him to go down those steps again. Inside, no skulls toppled from the shelf to shatter on the floor, and no rats scared me half out of my wits. The only noises were those I made with my pencils and brushes. The day passed quickly, and I returned the keys to the parsonage at about six.

"The little girl," I asked the parson, "did you find out how she died?"

"No, no. I sent for the doctor, but he lives over twenty miles away. He won't be here until tomorrow. All I know is that they found the child stone cold this morning. I didn't get to see her. I don't know why," he said mournfully, "but her parents wouldn't let me."

"It's very sad."

"It is indeed, Mr. Blake. It is indeed."

I returned to the inn and, out of respect for my hosts, who seemed to be very friendly with the family next door, I disappeared to my room as soon as I had finished my evening meal.

The next day I went to collect the keys for the third and last time. My detailed copy of the fresco was nearly finished, requiring only two or three hours more work. So you can imagine my dismay when I found that the parson was in no mood to give me the keys. He was pacing his study frantically, holding his hands over his temples. When he saw me, he stopped in his tracks, glared, and pointed an accusing finger.

"You and I, Mr. Blake, have done a very evil thing!"

Astonished by this remark, I didn't answer.

"Abraham Kelly is dead – *murdered* – and it's all our fault!"

"But... who is Abraham Kelly? And how can it be our fault?"

"He's the village blacksmith, found dead in his bed this morning, just like the child!" The parson sat down heavily in his armchair, on the point of tears.

"The doctor has just visited me. He has examined both corpses, and informed me of the cause of death. Strangulation! The child was strangled, Mr. Blake. I never thought I'd live to see Wetwaste at the mercy of that evil force once more!"

I was completely lost.

"Parson Higgins, with the greatest respect, I have no idea what you're talking about."

He looked at me bitterly.

"Let me tell you a story, Mr. Blake. Fifty years ago, when I was a young man just come to the village, there was a Lord of the Manor of Wetwaste. His name was Sir Roger Despard, and he..."

"Is there a Manor House in Wetwaste?" I interrupted.

"Not any more. When Sir Roger died the house was dismantled piece by piece, and all the stones were carried away. The gardens were dug up, grass was planted over the whole site, and now, not a trace of it remains."

"But... why?"

"Because Sir Roger Despard was the most vile,

inhuman monster that ever walked God's Earth. As I said, I arrived in this village as a young man fifty years ago. Sir Roger was nearing the end of a long life of evil and crime. Put bluntly, Mr. Blake, there isn't a person in Wetwaste who can't tell you of a parent or grandparent who has died at his hands. He dedicated his life to cruelty. Perhaps now, sir, you will forgive us our superstitions."

"Surely," I said, "the authorities would have been able to..."

"He *was* the authorities! He was the Justice of the Peace and the Member of Parliament! There was no police force in those days, so a tiny settlement like this was in the power of its lord completely."

I nodded, conceding the point reluctantly.

"In my first six months in this village," continued the parson, "I gradually learned about the horrific murders Sir Roger had committed. I was struggling with my conscience about what to do. But the decision was made for me when I received a summons to the Manor House. It was known that Sir Roger was on his deathbed. I was terrified to enter his murderous abode, but it was my holy duty to attend to him. Even the worst, most horrible sinners have been known to repent when they know their lives are near the end."

He sighed heavily, and gripped the edges of his chair. There was an expression of resignation and despair on his face.

"I still remember that building as clearly as if I had visited it yesterday, even though it was razed to the ground such a long time ago. Four stark towers stood at each corner, blackened by age. It was said that Sir Roger had dedicated each tower to a different method of torture.

"The front door was an immense iron structure which opened and shut on me like the door of a dungeon. Inside, Sir Roger's servant grabbed my arm roughly, and I thought I was a prisoner. The man was a huge, hulking brute who had never been known to speak, more like an animal than a human. He dragged me through endless dark corridors to the bedroom of Sir Roger Despard, where I found a terrifying scene. That room was festooned with weapons: all manner of knives, axes, clubs, cudgels, swords, muskets and pistols. It was like a monument to all the barbarous acts he had ever committed, a shrine to murder. And there in the middle of the room stood a vast four-poster bed, draped with curtains, behind which the monster lay dying."

"Could you see him?"

"No. But I could hear him. He was drawing long, gasping breaths. I held my Bible close to my chest, summoned up all my courage, and addressed him: 'The day of reckoning is upon you,' I said, in as clear and strong a voice as I could manage. 'Though you have lived a life of the utmost sin, yet the mercy of God is infinite to those who will repent, and accept Him as their Lord'.

"His tortured breathing became quieter. I flattered myself that there, on the very brink of death, he was perhaps reflecting on my words."

I watched the parson rise from his chair and walk to the window, to look at the bleak moor outside as though it could erase the memories.

"I was just deciding on what to say next when I heard what I can only describe as a *roar* of rage and agony. The curtain was pulled back, to reveal..."

He pressed his forehead against the latticed pane.

"... to reveal a man who looked more dead than alive. The nature of his disease and the inherent evil of his character had combined to make him resemble on the outside the monster that he was within. His ravaged flesh was mottled purple and grey. His eyes were enormous, so cold and unblinking, with tiny pupils and a great expanse of white around them which gave him a look of insanity. His mouth drooped on one side where it was permanently open, revealing yellow teeth. His lips were lumpy, almost black. It was like the face of some atrocious criminal already hanging from the gibbet. Either that, or it was the face of a devil."

As I have mentioned, I am not superstitious, but even I was appalled and fascinated by this description of Sir Roger Despard, half man and half monster, who had butchered and terrorized the people of Wetwaste. Now, as the parson turned away from the window to gaze at me unflinchingly, I waited in silence for the conclusion to his shocking story.

"He tried to sit up, groaning in agony, beckoning me with one long, bony finger. I moved closer, hoping that the extent of his suffering and the imminence of his own death had made him repent his life of murder.

" 'Speak,' I whispered.

" 'I... want... to... kill you!' he groaned.

"I am not ashamed to confess, Mr. Blake, that I stepped back in terror, lost my balance, and fell to the floor. As I struggled to my feet he laughed briefly, before collapsing into a fit of coughing.

" 'Fear not,' he whispered. 'I haven't the strength.'

" 'Renounce your sins,' I pleaded, 'or you will spend all eternity in the deepest pits of hell'.

"To which he answered curtly, with only one word: 'Good!'

"Terrified as I was, shaking like a leaf, the intensity of his evilness was spellbinding. He seemed at that moment to be a vision of pure wickedness.

" 'Is there nothing you regret?' I asked.

"An expression of agony crossed his already distorted features, an expression caused not by physical pain, but by mental torment.

" 'Yes.'

" 'Then tell me what it is,' I pleaded, slightly encouraged.

" 'Come closer, parson,' he hissed, beckoning again with his bony finger. 'My voice is weak.'

"I went as near as I dared, crouching down near his bed as he, half-propped up on his pillows, lay panting in exhaustion.

" 'Tell me what you regret,' I repeated.

" 'Parson, I cannot – I cannot bear the thought...'

" 'Yes?'

" 'Closer.'

"I did as he asked. He lurched nearer to me, his blackened lips now just inches from my ear.

" 'I cannot bear the thought that I shall never kill again!'

"The words petrified me, Mr. Blake. I was briefly rooted to the spot out of fear, then once again, as he collapsed into a fit of laughter and coughing, I leaped back. I stared at him, horrified that so much evil could reside in one man. As I watched, his coughing worsened, and his body became racked with shuddering fits. Death was only minutes away. He began to sob and rage, not because his life was leaving him, but because he couldn't kill any more.

" 'I *will* murder once more!' he bellowed.

"Summoning his strength, he threw himself out of the bed and fell to the floor by the wall. As I watched in loathing and disbelief, he grabbed a knife and began to..."

By now I could hardly contain my curiosity.

"What?" I breathed.

"And began to hack off his own hand!"

"Oh my God!"

"He hadn't the strength to do it, yet he was determined to do it, and as I watched, far too afraid to try to stop him, he hacked and hewed and slashed until it was done. At the end of his arm was nothing but a bleeding stump, and the severed hand lay next to it, twitching as he groaned.

" 'These are your last moments,' I whispered to him. 'Repent!'

"He looked at me, and the light in his eyes was already dying. But he had one last thing to say.

" 'I, Sir Roger Despard,' he hissed, 'leave this hand behind me, to murder and to maim...'

"Then he died, his eyes still fixed on my own."

The parson, exhausted, sat back down in his chair and rubbed his eyes wearily.

"Despard was buried in the crypt, and the hand with him, in a stone coffin at the back of the shelf of bones. The decision was made never to open up the crypt again. Nor would it have been, had you not arrived in Wetwaste, and had I not listened to you."

He gestured at me to leave, and turned away to the window again to contemplate the moor.

Though profoundly affected by the parson's appalling story, I didn't for one moment believe that the dead man's hand had 'escaped' from the crypt and committed two murders. The idea was ludicrous. The parson, however, had been adamant that he would not give me the keys. This was more than just annoying, it was illogical. If the hand had escaped – a ridiculous thought anyway – then it was now out of there. And if it really was out of there, locking the crypt wasn't going to make any difference.

I think I have already said that I always get what I want. As far as I was concerned, my copy of the fresco was nearly finished, and it would have been a crime not to complete it. So I decided to stay on in Wetwaste for another day or two, in the hope that I would somehow be able to get hold of the keys. It was by far the worst decision I have ever made.

I went to bed early that night, after a dreary day spent tramping around the countryside with Brin. I hadn't been asleep for very long when Brin woke me up. He was growling softly, as he sometimes did in his sleep. I told him to be quiet, then rolled over and buried my head under the sheets. Brin's growls continued, however, and the noise became steadily louder until it sounded so savage that I didn't recognize him as my own dog.

"Brin, shut up!" I called in the darkness.

He took no notice. I reached over to the bedside table and lit a candle. Was he going crazy? His eyes were bulging out of his head as he stared across the room at... at me. Less sure of myself than before, I ordered him for the final time to be quiet. He sprang at me. Shrinking back from his glinting teeth, I knocked the candle over and plunged us into darkness. The dog sent me sprawling, but he was moving so fast that he couldn't stop, and he went right over the top of me and onto the floor by the bed, snarling ferociously.

Convinced that the animal was demented, I jumped out of bed and rushed to the door in a futile attempt to escape. As I grabbed the handle, Brin's jaws seemed to close around my neck. I sank to my knees choking. I struggled to beat him off. I concentrated on staying conscious, and tried to pull at my throat to release the pressure. My arms flailed frantically at... at absolutely nothing.

No one – *no one* – can imagine my fear. It was far, far worse than the pain I could feel at my throat and in my lungs. My hands went to my neck, and closed on a slimy, vicious, cold thing... It wasn't my dog that was attacking me, it was Sir Roger's hand! I was being strangled! I keeled over in the darkness, only seconds away from death, frantically trying to rip the gruesome thing off my throat.

Brin must have launched himself at it again, because I was knocked over. For a moment I lay there, thrashing and twitching on the floor, the hand at my neck and Brin trying to pull it off. At last the vice-like grip released, and I fell flat on my back, exhausted. With huge, rasping gasps I drew the air back into my lungs. As the shock slowly began to recede, I felt pain take its place. I was weak and my head was spinning. If it had taken Brin another few seconds, I would have died.

Away from me the fight was continuing. Furniture and pots crashed to the floor, Brin snarled and snapped, then he gave a long and pathetic whine, almost a whimper, and silence fell. I lay in the darkness, half-dead, hearing nothing, until... what was it? That sound? Not quite a rustling noise, not quite a scraping sound, but something between the two. It sounded as if, at intervals of a few seconds, something was dragging itself across the floor.

I managed to get to my feet and stagger across to the bed. The table next to it was still standing, and I groped around for candles and matches, lighting a candle which threw its uneven light on...

It was the first time I had actually seen the hand. I screamed, out of my senses, maddened with terror. Though mauled and mangled, it was creeping across the floor toward me with terrible determination, bleeding black blood from its wounds. And behind the hand, somehow still alive despite his ripped throat, was Brin. In the last few seconds of his life, he was dragging himself after it, desperate to save me from its clutches.

At that point I totally lost control of myself, having some sort of fit or seizure which made me collapse to the floor, spluttering and sobbing. Unable to move, my bulging eyes fixed on the horrible thing that hauled itself ever nearer to my helpless body, I sank into unconsciousness in the certain expectation of death. The last thing I remember is the sight of the disgusting, wounded hand pulling itself slowly but surely to within inches of my neck. Its middle finger slowly extended, and a yellow, claw-like nail made contact with my skin. This was it. The terrible, terrifying touch of death.

Someone said: "Yes, he's coming to at last."

I opened my eyes. I was in a strange room, with a strange man leaning over me.

"What..." I croaked, then stopped, because the pain at my throat was unbearable.

"Don't speak," said the man. "I'm a doctor. Your throat has been crushed. You've been unconscious for four days, and you're lucky to be alive. This is Parson Higgins's house. Now you must rest."

It was more than a week before I could talk at all, and two weeks before Parson Higgins was allowed to speak to me at length.

"What happened?" I asked.

"The innkeeper's family could hear all the noise

coming from your room," he told me, "and they knew it was the hand. They were too frightened to help you, so they sent for me."

"You?" I whispered, looking at the frail old man perched on the end of my bed. "What did you... what did you find?"

"A gruesome scene, Mr. Blake: a dying man, a deadly hand, and a dead dog, all joined together in a chain of death. I thought you were probably dead. Your face was blue, and your tongue was hanging out. The thing was on you, its fingers compressing your neck, despite the fact that it was..."

"It was what?"

He paused.

"The severed hand was clenched between the jaws of the dead animal."

"Brin," I whispered, thinking how he must have made a final, agonizing attempt to save me

"I *had* to get that thing off you."

"What did you do?"

"Downstairs there was a fire in the grate. I ran down and picked up a red-hot coal with a pair of tongs. It was all I could think of. As soon as I went back upstairs I pressed the coal onto the back of the hand with all my strength, and..."

"What?"

"It, it *leaped* off your neck so violently that I tumbled over. Your poor dog, its teeth clamped on it, was pitched and tossed all around the room as the hand writhed and jumped in agony. Still holding the tongs, I managed to attack again, this time pressing the coal into the palm. Its evil fingers closed around it, and there was the sweet, sickly smell of flesh melting and fusing with the coal. The hand knocked against the floor, hard – six, seven, eight times – then all was still."

Every day I thank God that I'm still alive, and I remember Brin, who sacrificed his life for mine. It's been ten years since he died. Even in death it proved to be impossible to release the hand from his teeth, so when the hand, charred and blackened, was once again locked in the crypt, Brin had to go with it.

I still bear the ugly, livid marks of strangulation on my throat: five purple-black marks, four on one side, one on the other. They have never faded. Is it any wonder that I always wear high collars?

The Cat

"Doggy," my brother said, pointing at the cat which was sitting on the kitchen step.

My brother's name is Peter. He is only two and a half years old, which is thirteen years younger than me. I was preparing his breakfast, and because it was a sunny day I'd opened the back door.

"Cat," I said, "*cat*."

"Cat."

"Good boy."

There was something I didn't like about that cat. It was a horrible, dirty stray, unusually large and muscular, with shabby, dark-grey fur and the most astonishing orange eyes that stared right through me.

"Shoo!" I called.

It stayed exactly where it was, regarding me with an almost human expression of amused contempt.

"Cat! Cat, cat, cat!" Peter shouted excitedly.

"Good heavens, Lizzie, what's all the noise?" said my mother as she came into the room. "Goodness, what an enormous cat! Shall we give it some milk?"

"But it probably has fleas, mother."

"Nonsense dear, it's just a little dirty. You would be too if you didn't have anywhere to live."

She went into the larder to get the milk. Meanwhile, as I looked on uneasily, the cat stalked up to Peter.

"It's a real bruiser," I said.

Peter started to laugh happily, reaching out to pat the animal. To my surprise, it put up with his clumsy buffetings, and remained quite calm even when Peter pulled its fur. I crouched down to stroke the animal myself, not to make friends with it but to check if it had fleas. I was relieved to see that it didn't.

"Then Bruiser is what we shall call him," mother announced, placing a saucer of milk before him.

The animal sniffed it warily, then turned its nose up at it.

"I've never met a cat that didn't like milk," mother said. "Do you think it would prefer sardines?"

"I'm sure it would," I said indignantly. "In fact why doesn't it go the whole hog and just move in? After all, there's lots of space."

Although we are not very poor, we are certainly not rich, and our tiny house has only four rooms, a living room, a kitchen and two small bedrooms.

"Don't be silly, dear," my mother trilled from the larder, where she was busy looking for the sardines.

Bruiser didn't like sardines either. Nor did he like cheese, giblets, liver or trout. I know this because he started to visit us every morning, and each time my mother would try to get him to eat something different. He never even tasted anything.

"What a strange creature," mother concluded one morning. "He doesn't seem to eat at all. The only thing he's interested in is Peter."

It was true that Bruiser and Peter had become the best of friends. Every morning now, when I carried Peter down the stairs, he would shout "Cat! Cat!", or sometimes even "Bwoozer! Bwoozer!", and he would then bawl nonstop until I let the cat in. If Bruiser had been kept waiting outside, he used to look at me in an odd way when he entered. I know it probably sounds stupid, but I'm hardly exaggerating when I describe the look on that animal's face as one of smirking insolence.

One morning the cat, as usual, was being "stroked" by my brother, which involved having his fur pulled.

"He's incredibly placid, and Peter loves him," I said, "but I still don't like him."

"What a nasty thing to say to Bruiser," said mother, crouching down next to Peter to stroke the cat. "How can she be so nasty to you?"

It probably took less than a second. Mother wears a chain around her neck with a cross on it. As she bent forward to stroke the cat, the cross slipped out of her dress and knocked against Bruiser's shoulder. Bruiser *yowled*, lashing out wildly with one of his claws as he leaped away. My mother gave a little scream of fright.

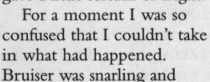

For a moment I was so confused that I couldn't take in what had happened. Bruiser was snarling and spitting under the kitchen table. My mother, frozen in surprise, was still bending forward, the cross dangling from her neck, and Peter...

"Peter!"

There were scratch marks from his left eye all the way down to his chin. Little beads of blood began to emerge. Only just becoming aware of the pain, he began to cry.

"*Shoo!*" I shouted at Bruiser furiously, "*Shoo!*", and I chased him out of the kitchen. He fled across the little yard and jumped onto the high wall at the back. He stopped to look back at me. From inside the house I could hear Peter crying, and my mother's fruitless attempts to comfort him. I am not normally cruel to animals, but I was so angry that I wanted to scare Bruiser away.

"You horrible thing!" I shouted, picking up a big stone and hurling it at him.

I don't think I expected to hit the target, and in fact I put my hand to my mouth in dismay when the stone hit Bruiser full on the body. I had thrown with such force that it nearly knocked him off the wall. To my amazement, instead of howling in pain like any other cat would and making a terrified escape, Bruiser stayed exactly where he was. He didn't even make a noise. He simply looked down at the stone as it fell to the ground, more in curiosity than in shock. And then he slowly raised his head once more, and gazed at me.

It wasn't the stare of an ordinary animal. I swear to God that his strange orange eyes were so full of loathing that I was scared he was going to pounce on me. I stepped back, instinctively, just in case. But Bruiser, after a few more moments of staring at me with his terrifying glare, sauntered along the wall and disappeared over the other side.

After all that, you would have thought that Bruiser would have found a new family to adopt him. We never let him in the house again, and we tried to make sure that we didn't leave the doors open, so that he couldn't slip in unnoticed.

My mother and I were deliberately unfriendly to him – almost mean – but that didn't seem to stop him from hanging around. He was always there. If we were in the kitchen, he was sure to be sitting on the back wall, and if we were in the living room at the front of the house, he often sat in the cherry tree that was at the side of the tiny lawn. Sometimes he sat in the middle of the lawn itself, staring intently into the house.

I started to hate Bruiser, to hate him passionately without really knowing why. He wasn't like ordinary cats that just bask in the sun; he *watched*. His eyes followed us around, especially Peter. Sometimes, if I had just brought Peter into the living room, I'd see Bruiser stand up in the cherry tree and arch his back. It gave me the creeps. Despite my mother's scolding I even started to close the curtains in the daytime, just so that I wouldn't have to look at him. I know this sounds strange, but I couldn't bear the sight of him.

"I wish I'd never set eyes on that animal," my mother sighed one day. "I had to go right up to him just now, and shout, and even then he ambled away, as calm as you please."

We were hanging out some washing in the back yard. I'd just come through the house from the front where I'd been weeding. Peter was upstairs having his usual afternoon nap.

"What do you think he wants from us?" I said.

"What do you mean, *wants* from us?" my mother asked. "He doesn't want anything. He's just a cat."

"Is he?" I asked.

"What a strange girl you are sometimes," mother said, picking up the empty linen basket and going back into the house.

Mother is right, I thought with a sigh. *A cat is just, well... a cat.*

"Lizzie, you left the front door open!" mother called from inside.

"Oh, sorry."

A dull thud indicated that she had shut it. I sat down on the doorstep and closed my eyes, enjoying the feel of the sun on my face, and the smell of the newly-washed clothes billowing in the breeze. I was hoping to visit one of my friends once all the housework was done, and maybe...

A scream, a scream of disbelief and panic, shattered my thoughts.

"Mother!" I shouted, rushing into the house, "mother, what is it?"

"Oh Lizzie!" she shrieked.

She was upstairs. I hurtled up the stairs and burst into the room. Mother was standing by Peter's bed, wringing her hands. It was empty.

"Where is he?" I implored her, half out of my wits with worry.

She had no answer but pitiful sobs. I collapsed by the bed, screaming his name over and over again. And then I saw that the bed wasn't empty.

Bizarrely and inexplicably, a tiny frightened animal was looking up at us. It was a little brown kitten.

"Oh mother, where's Peter, where's Peter?"

"Run to the police station Lizzie. Tell them that Peter's been, been *taken*," she wailed, "and I'll start looking for him."

"But, but – how did this kitten..."

"*Go!*" she yelled.

The police mounted a huge search party, but Peter wasn't found. After the first week, the police search was called off. After two weeks, even mother and I didn't go out looking for him any more. Somehow, we knew that my brother was gone.

We were utterly heartbroken. Mother in particular found things impossible. She gave up on life. Once she had been so cheerful and busy, but now she was incapable of anything but grieving. She didn't get up in the mornings unless I nagged and nagged her, and when she finally did get up it was only to sit in the living room, rocking to and fro in her chair. When it was time to go to bed the same thing would happen in reverse, and if I didn't bully her she wouldn't go to bed at all, but would sit there through the night, dozing fitfully.

For a time, my mother's breakdown helped me. I had to look after her, I had to do everything for her, and so I was kept busy. Nothing could take away the inconsolable ache in my heart, but my mother needed me so much that there simply wasn't time to let grief destroy me.

The evenings were the worst, though, when there was no more work, when I'd run out of ways to try to comfort mother, and had nothing to do but wait until it was time to go to bed. I remember how long those evenings seemed, listening to her weeping in the living room, while I sat in the kitchen. I tried devoting myself to looking after the little kitten. It was certainly an improvement on Bruiser, who seemed to have gone for good. It was a sweet little creature, lively and mischievous. I couldn't explain where it had come from, but I thought that it deserved to be cared for. Perhaps there was a part of me pretending it was Peter.

It was only when the kitten fell ill that I started to despair myself. I'd managed to hold myself together through the worst tragedy I could imagine, and then

I fell to pieces when a kitten became sick. For the first two or three weeks it was all right, but it started to have difficulty eating. Although it would drink the milk I put in front of it, and eat the minced fish, it obviously didn't like it much, and sometimes it was sick. This situation got worse until in the end the kitten wouldn't eat at all, even though it was starving to death.

"Please, please take some milk," I whispered to it one night.

I was holding it in the palms of my hands. It looked up at me, piteously, mewing in a high-pitched squeak as I gently put it down by the saucer. It was so weak that it nearly fell over, but it sniffed at the milk. For a moment my hopes were raised. But it turned away, took a few steps, and then curled up miserably. I just put my head in my hands, and wept.

The next evening I decided I had to get out by myself. I felt that I had been cooped up for so long that I was in danger of going insane. I left mother in the living room with the kitten, which was now close to death, promising that I would be home before it got dark.

It had been a hot day. It was nearly eight o'clock but the sun was still quite fierce, so I took my parasol. I made my way slowly down the street, across the main road and to the park. All I could think about was Peter, how much I missed him, how he was gone forever. I think I was actually crying as I shuffled along the path, past the flower beds.

Everyone seemed so happy: the couples walking arm in arm, the old people on the park benches soaking up the heat, and most of all the children — running, shouting, and laughing. I could hardly bear to watch them, so I headed for the other side of the park, the quieter, wilder part, and walked around the lake. The ducks in the water pursued me, hoping for bread. I didn't have any. I didn't want the ducks to follow me. I wanted... I just wanted Peter to come back to us.

"Oh, go away!" I suddenly shouted at the ducks, taking myself, and them, by surprise.

They scattered in a quacking, splashing panic, leaving me standing at the edge of the lake feeling guilty. I looked around and saw, not very far away, a man observing me curiously, and, beyond him, a cluster of giggling children. What was I doing, shouting at ducks in a park? Was I losing my mind? I lowered the parasol over my face and hurried away, away from the prying eyes of people, to the shelter of the trees.

I was so very tired, absolutely exhausted after the weeks of heartache and hard work. I just collapsed under the shade of an enormous chestnut tree, put my head on my arm, and fell asleep.

I don't know what time it was when I woke up – late, very late. The moon was almost full, casting long moon-shadows of the trees over the grass. I sat up, shivering and stiff, and thought about mother – I'd said I wouldn't be long; she'd be worried to death! I grabbed my parasol, stood up and rushed off.

I ran out of the trees, around the lake and back into the more formal part of the park, along the path that leads to the big square with the statue of the Queen in the middle. It was when I reached the statue that I stopped in my tracks.

I saw Bruiser. It was the first time I'd seen him since Peter went missing. He seemed meaner than ever under the moon's glimmering light. I took a few steps back and hid behind the statue, feeling unnacountably terrified of him. He was moving delicately around the path that circled the statue, placing one foot slowly in front of the other, stopping to sniff the air... he was *stalking*.

With great caution I moved around the statue, my hands on the cold granite plinth, wondering what animal the cat was hunting. Then I saw a homeless man on a park bench. He was lying down, with his coat bundled up for a pillow, and a bottle of wine in a paper bag on the ground. I watched, fascinated and puzzled, as Bruiser carefully moved closer and closer to him.

The man let out a loud, long snore and turned over. Bruiser paused, waited for a few moments, continued to advance. I didn't know what to think. Was Bruiser, a *cat*, going to attack a man? Surely it wasn't possible.

By this time Bruiser had reached the bench and gone behind it. He jumped nimbly and silently onto the back of it and looked down at the sleeping man under him. He raised his head and stared at the moon for a few moments, his ears flattening against his skull and the fur standing up on his back. His jaws opened wide, to reveal the sharp teeth glinting within...

Then I saw something that was so horrible, so unimaginable, that I nearly fainted. The animal's teeth started to grow, its head got bigger, its whole body cracked and creaked and expanded, transforming until, in less than five seconds, Bruiser had changed into a man, no, not a man, a vampire!

It – he – looked down at his prey, slavering with anticipation, his orange eyes dancing with delight, and then he held out his hands in front of him, uncurling the long fingers to reveal sharp, curving nails. The man moaned in his sleep. I tried to scream, to wake him up, but I was speechless with shock, and the vampire fell on him so quickly and savagely that nothing could have saved him. A scream rang through the park as sharp teeth punctured the old man's neck. His body shuddered. Disbelief and shock merged together in my mind, making me dizzy, making me lurch back.

I woke up, sprawled on the cold stone path by the statue. I had fainted. I staggered to my feet and looked across to the bench. The vampire had gone, and the man was nowhere to be seen. In his place, mewing piteously, was a tabby cat.

I rushed over to the animal, amazed and appalled, as all the pieces of the puzzle fell into place: the same thing had happened to Peter! He hadn't disappeared, he'd been attacked by that foul vampire-cat! The kitten, the dying kitten, was Peter! I let out a cry of agony as I started to run home, as fast as I could, faster than I had ever run in my life. A new and even more shocking realization suddenly dawned on me: the kitten wouldn't drink milk for the same reason that Bruiser had refused it – it needed blood! Peter himself was a vampire-cat, and he was alone in the house with my mother!

When I reached the garden gate I came to a sudden halt and stared. A wave of pure terror washed over me. Bruiser was sitting on the window ledge. The curtains were open, and inside, fast asleep, was my mother. All I could see of her was her head slumped against the settee – and stalking along the back of the settee, as Bruiser watched, was the kitten. It was still tiny, but now its face was distorted with its hunger for blood. The fur bristled on its body, its claws were extended, and its jaws slowly opened to reveal the fangs of a vampire growing rapidly inside its mouth.

It sickened me to know that this thing, this baby vampire, was Peter. I imagined it transforming – just as I had seen Bruiser transform himself earlier – into a monstrous version of my brother. Crying out in anger and despair, I scrabbled at the ground until my fingers closed around a stone. I picked it up and hurled it at the window.

After that, everything seemed to happen in slow motion. I saw the kitten grow, swelling like a balloon being steadily blown up, preparing to strike at my mother's throat. I saw Bruiser spin around on the window ledge to glare at me in fury. I saw the stone smash into the window pane with a deafening crash. Glass shattered on the ground – fragments and great jagged shards of it. The next thing I knew, my mother was screaming in the living room, the vampire-kitten had disappeared from view, and Bruiser was hissing with hate.

Then Bruiser's body bulged and thickened. It became the size of a big dog, and dropped down to the ground to stand up on its two back legs. It was still growing, turning into a beast that was half man and half animal, its fur becoming a dark and swirling cloak until there, in front of me, spitting with rage, was the fully-formed vampire I had seen in the park only minutes before. My heart almost stopped with fright. I backed away, helplessly, unable to take my gaze away from the furious expression on the creature's face.

Only his eyes remained cat-like, a curious shade of orange with thin black slits instead of pupils. His face was twisted in anger, and his pallid skin had a slight grey tinge, while his deadly fangs curled down over his lower lip.

"You fool!" he hissed. His voice was a strange combination of a screech and a sigh.

"Do you dare to think that you can defy my will? I, who have lived for over five hundred years, and have sucked the blood of a thousand times that many victims? Come here," he spat, "and submit to your death. Prepare to become a member of the legions of darkness!"

At that moment I could neither run away nor do as he ordered. My legs were trembling so violently that it was impossible to move.

"Leave us alone!" I managed to shriek. "Please, leave us alone!"

He laughed. His sly face crinkled up with mirth, and his deadly fangs were all too visible.

"Leave you alone? But you don't understand – there are two of you left! I want you to be a little family of vampires. There's nothing you can do to protect yourselves. You must accept your fate. Come here."

It felt as if someone had tied lead weights to my feet when I walked up to him. He smiled with a fiendish pleasure. I stood in front of him, and his lip curled in contempt. We stayed like that for a short time, watching one another intently. From the inside of the house I could hear my mother. She was whimpering in shock.

"Are you ready to die?" the vampire whispered.

I nodded. I felt his hands or claws tighten on my shoulders as he threw his head back and opened his mouth wide. A disgusting hissing noise came out of it. And then, suddenly, I realised what I had to do. It still felt as if I was in a trance, but somehow I found my strength. At the exact moment that his mouth lowered onto my neck, using all my power, I plunged my parasol between his jaws. He roared with rage and struck me to the ground. It was a hugely powerful blow that nearly knocked me unconscious. As I lay dazed on the ground, I could hear him coughing and gagging as he tried to wrench the parasol free. In those few seconds, I understood exactly what I had to do next.

"Mother!" I screamed, "your cross! I need your cross!" My mother was incapable of responding.

I scrambled to my feet and tried to escape. But the vampire dealt me another blow that catapulted me against the house. I lay draped over the ledge of the broken window, winded, helpless and terrified. This time there was to be no second chance. Beside himself with fury, the vampire sprang on me and pulled my head back by the hair to expose my neck. I looked up at the jagged glass that was hanging from the top of the window frame, thinking I was going to die. I closed my eyes and waited.

Why did he take so long? Was he relishing the prospect of tasting my blood? Does time slow down at the moment of death? I heard a kind of whistling noise, a harsh intake of breath, and then his vice-like grip released. I opened my eyes in amazement and saw the vampire was lurching backward, holding onto a great dagger of glass that was sticking out of his chest. It had fallen from the window frame above. It had gone straight into his back, pierced his heart and come out of the other side.

The look on that monster's face is beyond description – outrage, disbelief, shock, these words only hint at it. He collapsed to his knees.

"You..." he whispered.

I'll never know what he was going to say. His hands clutched tightly at the glass protruding from his body, so that the blood from his heart mingled with the blood from his fingers. The orange light of his eyes died in front of my gaze. He fell onto his back. The ground pushed the dagger of glass, red and gleaming, deeper through his body. The wound started to smoke. Within seconds the vampire was consumed by fire, leaving nothing but a scorched black mark on the ground and a few wisps of foul-smelling smoke.

I fell down, sobbing hysterically. I've no idea how long I stayed like that. All I know is that at some stage I became aware that my mother was saying, "Peter, Peter," over and over again, and at the same time I heard a sound that I thought I would never hear again... Peter's crying.

"Peter!" I shouted, scrambling to my feet.

My mother was holding him in her arms, clutching him as if she would never let him out of her sight again. The vampire was dead, and his victim had been returned to us.

The Beast From Nowhere

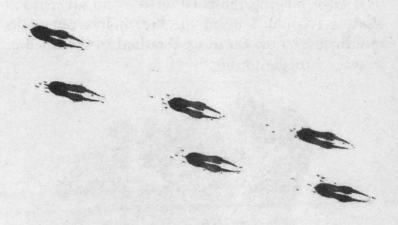

In that room, on that night, at twelve o'clock, something unimaginable happened to me. The room was an ordinary room, with a bed, a chest of drawers, a cupboard, and a desk under the window. The day had been ordinary, too. I had gone to work and come home again. I had eaten my supper as usual. And I went to bed without the slightest reason for thinking that something extraordinary was about to happen. I turned the gas lamp off, then rolled onto my back, letting out a tired sigh into the darkness. Perhaps I yawned. I'm not sure. And then it happened. It dropped onto me from above, as though it had been clinging to the ceiling, and the next instant two bony hands were at my throat and squeezing tight.

I heard myself choking as I tried to pull its arms away. I was suddenly fighting for my life. Unable to release the murderous grip of the creature that was throttling me, I wrapped my arms around its body – its strange, bulging, muscular torso – and squeezed as hard as I could. I heard the breath hiss out of its mouth, just by my ear, as we thrashed and writhed in a savage struggle for life.

I was suffocating. My eyes felt as if they were being pushed out of my face from the inside, and I no longer had enough breath even to splutter when, seconds away from unconsciousness, the grip on my neck relaxed.

We rolled apart. I had time to take in a gasping lungful of air before it attacked again. It slashed me with its claws and sank its sharp teeth into my shoulders and neck. Although it seemed to be slightly smaller than me, it was ferociously strong.

It was a fight of awful intensity. Immersed in the darkness, repulsed by the feel of the beast's skin, I tried to fend it off without stopping to think about it. Ignorant of what thing was so intent on killing me, I simply struggled to survive. Once more we rolled on the floor in a flailing tussle.

At last, after an exhausting fight, I managed to pin my assailant down beneath me by placing my knee on its chest and putting all my weight on it. It thrashed and writhed, but after a while it stopped struggling. I could feel its heart throbbing violently. It was as tired as I was.

There was a large handkerchief on the chair nearby. Keeping the thing pinned under me, despite its renewed attempts to get away, I used the handkerchief to tie up its wrists. I felt safer then, although it was still tiring to hold the creature down. Still keeping my knee on its chest, I dragged it awkwardly across the room to the bedside table. Quick as lightning, I released my grip and turned the lamp on.

The unimaginable had already happened once. Now it happened again. I let out a shriek, not so much of terror, though I was terrified, but of dismay and disbelief. There was a beast pinned to the ground under me. I could feel its chest rising and falling, I could hear its horrible rasping breath, and I could see the handkerchief that bound its wrists together – but I couldn't see *it!*

It was in this situation that David, my housemate, found me when he ran into the room.

He said, "What's the matter? Why are you bleeding?" I must have presented an unnerving sight. I was moaning in terror, and struggling desperately with an assailant that he couldn't see.

"For God's sake help me," I pleaded, "it nearly killed me, I can't hold it down for much longer!"

He stared at me.

"*Help me!*" I shouted

"I'll get a doctor."

"No, please!" I cried. "Just – come here, David!"

As soon as he was close enough, I grabbed his hand firmly and pressed it down on the thing's chest. He froze in horror, and the flesh on his face quivered. Then his mouth opened to scream, but no sound came out. I let go of his wrist and he shot back, away from me and the thing, to huddle in a corner of the room.

"What – what is it? What's there?"

"I don't know."

"It's invisible!" David suddenly bellowed, so loudly that it would have been funny if it hadn't been true.

"For pity's sake, for the last time, *help me!*" I begged him, desperately.

At last he seemed to understand how worn out I was. He ran from the room, returning shortly with a ball of yellow twine. We trussed the beast up tightly. Once that was done, we were left with a network of string wrapped around what was, to all intents and purposes, a vacant space. The thing strained to break free from its prison of string.

"Harry," David said eventually. "This is awful."

"Yes."

"It's also impossible."

I stretched out on the floor, just yards from the panting thing itself, and looked up at the ceiling.

"Glass is transparent," I said.

"But you can still see it."

"You can't see air."

"But air doesn't breathe, air doesn't live. Air," he said fiercely, "doesn't have teeth!"

"What shall we do?" I asked.

We watched over it into the night, talking about what to do. We didn't dare leave it for a moment.

"Listen," David whispered after a few hours.

The thing was breathing deeply and slowly. It had fallen asleep.

"Do you think you can guard it on your own for an hour or two?" David said.

"I suppose so, although I'd rather not. Why?"

"I need to get some equipment. I've thought of a way of finding out what it looks like."

"It doesn't look like anything. It's invisible."

"But it has a shape," he replied, "so it must look like something. I'll be back soon."

"David, wait!" I hissed, suddenly frightened to be left alone with the thing that had tried to kill me, but David was already halfway out of the door.

When he returned about an hour later, he had two big buckets of plaster of Paris with him. I watched him in astonishment as he gave the plaster a final stir. I knew what he intended to do, but I couldn't believe that it was possible.

"You're not going to take a plastercast of it?"

"I am."

"But it will wake up!"

"No it won't."

"And it's covered in string."

"I'm going to cut the string off."

I looked at him as if he were a complete idiot. He smiled at me, and took a small bottle of liquid from his jacket pocket.

"Chloroform," he said.

He poured some chloroform onto his handkerchief, and placed it over where he thought the creature's nose was. It woke up instantly and began to struggle, but David pressed down hard, and within a few seconds the string stopped moving. It had lost consciousness.

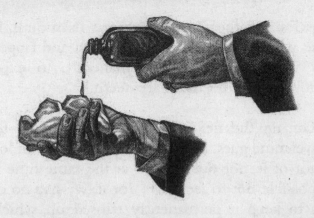

David dripped some more chloroform onto the handkerchief.

"Better safe than sorry," he said, grimly.

When we had cut the strings off, I felt very vulnerable; at least we could see where the thing was before. Now there was nothing to say that it existed but the sound of its breathing.

"You crouch by its head," David told me, "and listen. If there's the slightest sign that it's waking up, give it some more chloroform.

Working from the creature's feet up, he started to cover it with a thick layer of plaster of Paris.

By lunchtime the next day David had created a full-size wax model. I have never seen, nor hope to see again, a more hideous beast. It wasn't particularly tall, about the size of a twelve-year-old boy, but its huge, muscular arms were nearly as long as its body. It had two-toed feet, with long, curling claws. The torso was frightening, bulbous and bursting with muscles, but the worst thing was its mouth. It was little wonder that my flesh was torn and ripped: the lips were drawn back permanently, to expose a vicious row of needle-sharp teeth.

During the next few days our attitude to our unwelcome guest changed. Though we never lost our terror of it, nor our disgust, at the same time it was impossible not to feel sorry for it. We had no choice but to keep it permanently trussed up, which was little short of torture. And it was starving to death.

"If it won't take soup then it won't take anything," David said, watching me as I gingerly tried to feed it with vegetable broth. We had already tried it with milk, bread, fruit, meat and eggs.

"You don't think it's the string?" I asked. "Perhaps it can't open its mouth enough."

David felt over the creature's face carefully. He took out a pocket knife and delicately cut through a couple of knots, creating a hole where he thought the mouth was.

"Try it now," he said.

I leaned forward again, a spoon of hot soup in one hand, the other hand cautiously feeling for its mouth.

"I think we'll be successful this time," David said, "I think it was just..."

"*AAH!*" I yelled.

The thing had given a sudden lurch and now my wrist was in its mouth! Its teeth had punctured my skin and, as I looked down in disgust and tried in vain to pull my arm away, thin streams of blood flowed out of my wrist, as though being sucked up through invisible straws.

"My God," David whispered.

The creature was swallowing and gulping, and we saw my blood apparently floating in thin air as it passed from its mouth to its throat and down to its stomach. Once in the stomach it faded and within a few seconds became invisible.

"*Get it off me!*" I wailed.

David grabbed my arm and tried to free it, but this just made me scream in pain. The blood was now streaming out of my veins and I was starting to feel faint. The shock was more than I could bear. David took control of the situation.

"Brace yourself," he told me.

Then, with all his strength, he *wrenched* my arm away. There was a brittle snapping noise – some of the creature's teeth breaking off – immediately drowned out by my howl of agony and shock. My arm was free, but a chunk of flesh was missing, attached to the broken teeth of the thing. Blood started to spurt from the wound, and David quickly tied a tourniquet around my upper arm to reduce the flow, before binding the wound itself.

"Now we know what it feeds on," he said with a shudder. "Human blood."

We had a long discussion about what to do. We wanted to tell someone, but at the same time we were worried about what might happen. If the newspapers heard of the story, there could be a general panic.

"Surely the safest thing to do is to kill it," I suggested eventually.

"We can't do that," David whispered. "Don't you understand that this is the most incredible mystery the world has ever known? We have to get to the bottom of it!"

"But how?"

"I've never known anything like it!" Dr. Higginson announced, beside himself with excitement. He was tracing the contours of the creature's body with trembling hands.

Dr. Stephen Higginson was David's uncle. He was a scientist at the university, an expert in biology and natural history. We had asked him to visit us without telling him why, worried that if we had told him about the strange creature he simply wouldn't have believed us.

"How do you explain it?" I asked.

"Although *I* can't explain it, I'm sure it *can* be explained," he said, rather enigmatically. "That, my friend, is one of the fundamental assumptions underlying all science."

"It's hardly breathing any more," David said.

The doctor put his ear to the creature's chest.

"Hmm. Very faint."

"How long will it last?" I asked.

Dr. Higginson didn't answer. He was frowning in concentration, utterly absorbed in his thoughts.

"Extraordinary," he said again.

"What?"

"It's the heart, and the whole respiratory mechanism. It seems to work in a completely different way from the human system. Fascinating."

"What do you want to do?"

"I'd like to subject it to some laboratory experiments. There are certain small marine animals that are largely transparent, and I'd like to compare their tissues. And yet..."

"What?"

"*Invisible* organic matter is an entirely different proposition from transparent organic matter." He bent down and put his ear to the thing's chest again. "Extraordinary. What does it feed on?"

There was an awkward pause.

"Blood. Human blood."

"*What?*"

"That's why we've been so worried about what might happen if it escapes, or gets into the wrong hands," David explained.

"It's absolutely essential," the doctor said decisively, "to get this creature into a controlled and safe environment, under proper scientific supervision."

"But people would find out about it if you took it to the university. There could be a mass panic."

"Perhaps," said the doctor, "we could transfer it to my own private laboratory. Only us three need know.

Of course, once I've established what it is and why it's invisible..."

Somehow, I couldn't help thinking that he was imagining the fame and glory he would receive should he solve the mystery.

When darkness fell we bundled the beast into a blanket and smuggled it into Dr. Higginson's house, which was about half a mile away. The doctor's servants, a husband and wife named Mr. and Mrs. Trewin, had been given the evening off. Once in the house we carried the thing down to the laboratory in the basement. There was a heavy trapdoor that Dr. Higginson promised to keep locked. We left him to his experiments. That night I slept soundly in my bed for the first time since the creature had arrived, though my dreams were vivid and frightening.

I awoke refreshed and with a new sense of interest in the case. David seemed to feel the same. As soon as we had finished our breakfast we made our way across the city to the doctor's house. It was only as we stood on his doorstep, waiting for the door to be answered, that I felt the first chill of foreboding. Something was definitely wrong.

"It's taking a long time."

"Perhaps the servants are still in bed after their night off," David said. "He lets them get away with far too much."

I rang the bell again but there was still no answer.

"I don't suppose the door is already open," suggested David, turning the handle. "Ah. No."

"Let's walk around the back."

The doctor's house was a large villa set in its own grounds. David and I climbed over the wall at the back and walked up to the rear of the house through the trees. It was as we came onto the lawn that David let out a cry of surprise.

"Look at the door!"

It was smashed to pieces. A single piece of wood was hanging pathetically from the hinges.

"Come on!"

We rushed inside and made our way to the trapdoor. I felt sick with dismay at what I saw: a hole had been smashed through the middle of it. David frantically pulled away the broken pieces of wood, and climbed down the ladder into the laboratory.

I heard his sharp intake of breath before I too witnessed the scene of desolation below: broken glass, upturned furniture, pools of chemicals on the floor. It was as if a tornado had hit the room.

"Look," David said grimly, holding up some shreds of yellow twine.

"I can't believe he untied it."

"He must have done."

"But *why?*"

My friend shrugged sadly.

"His scientific curiosity must have overwhelmed him."

We found the doctor under an overturned laboratory bench. I'll never forget what he looked like. Agony was etched on his face. At his throat was a neat row of small holes. What shocked me more than anything, however, was that he was almost snow-white. Even his lips were white. The creature had sucked every last drop of blood out of his body.

"The *fool!*" David exclaimed.

"You don't think – you don't think it's still here?"

We looked around uneasily. There were a few footprints in blood, but they didn't lead anywhere. It was impossible to know if it had disappeared forever into the streets of the city, or was standing only yards away from us, or if it was elsewhere in the house.

"The servants!" I suddenly exclaimed. "We ought to check that they're all right."

"Whatever we do," David said, as we made our way back up the steps and into the house, "we must stick together."

I was only too ready to agree.

Mr. and Mrs. Trewin filled the roles of cook, butler, housekeeper, handyman and gardener. I was hoping against hope that they hadn't been in the house when the beast escaped; they were an elderly couple, who wouldn't have stood a chance.

With me in the lead, we quickly checked the living room and the dining room – there was nothing out of the ordinary in either – before we rushed to the servants' quarters. We raced through the hall to the kitchen, but even before I entered I could see, through the doorway, a pair of legs sticking out from under the kitchen table. Mrs. Trewin had suffered the same fate as the doctor, although her skin wasn't as snow-white. Instead of a neat row of holes on her neck, her throat showed the evidence of a swift, savage attack.

"This blood," David said, kneeling at her side. "It's fresh. She wasn't killed last night. She was killed this morning."

I picked up a large kitchen knife that was lying on the table.

"What shall we do?" I asked.

At that moment there was a noise. David and I looked at each other. It sounded like something had been knocked over in a nearby room.

"The pantry," he whispered, pointing to a door.

He picked up a knife too. We tiptoed over to the pantry door. My heart was pounding. My legs felt wobbly. I had no idea about what we intended to do, but I was aware that our lives were in great danger. Before I knew it, David had flung the door open, and we were filling the doorway, holding our knives at the ready. We had a split second to take in what was happening. At our feet, lying in the narrow corridor between rows of food-packed shelves, was Mr. Trewin. He was on his back, and his hands were grappling with something just above his neck. Blood seeped in thin streams from his throat into thin air. David hurled himself onto the invisible thing, but it must have sprung away at the same time, because David landed heavily on Mr. Trewin with nothing in between them.

"Don't let it get out!" David shouted, sprawled on the floor.

I thought I saw a hazy red blob coming at me, suspended in the air: it was the fresh blood in the creature's stomach. I panicked. Shrieking in terror, I wildly slashed at the air in front of me. By chance my knife ripped into a big bag of flour on a shelf. It was like a little explosion. Suddenly there was flour everywhere. It swirled in dense clouds, covering me, the shelves, David, the beast...

Looking like the visible ghost of its invisible self, it launched itself at me, and I went tumbling back into the kitchen with the beast on top of me. I was screaming in panic and trying to stab it with my knife, but my arm was pinned down by its weight. I heard it snorting and grunting horribly in my ear as it attempted to sink its teeth into my neck. I think I was seconds away from being killed when it made a noise I have never heard before, one which I can't even describe but which was so loud that it deafened me. David was standing above us, stabbing it again and again between its shoulders. Then it was still. Its dead weight lay on top of me, as David, panting, looked down.

"Get it off me," I groaned.

He shoved it roughly, and it rolled onto the floor in a cloud of white powder. I just lay there on the floor, exhausted. David went back into the pantry to tend to Mr. Trewin, but he came out almost immediately.

"He's dead."

I didn't reply.

"Are you all right?"

He pulled me up, and we looked down at the beast that had come from nowhere to claim three lives. It was still sprinkled with a light covering of flour, but we could see straight through it. It was as if we were looking through frosted glass.

"The police won't believe their eyes," I said.

For a minute, maybe more, we continued to gaze at the creature, until David said, "What's going on? What's happening?"

"What do you mean?"

"Where's it — where's it going?"

It was gradually disappearing. The flour on its

body floated gently to the floor. I rushed to the pantry and gathered up more flour in my hands, and hurled it at the creature, but there was hardly any creature left. It was as though the thing were melting or dissolving into nothing. David got down on his knees and scrabbled around on the floor.

"It's not there!" he cried, almost in despair.

It was subject to laws of biology different from ours. Was it even now re-forming somewhere else, in another place or another world? Or did its disappearance signify that it was truly dead? How could we ever know? All that we could be sure of was that we were left alone with three dead bodies, and the certain knowledge that no one would believe us when we tried to explain how they died.

An Original Revenge

Charles Gratmar was a solitary, dreamy young man. Everyone agreed he should never have joined the army. At the garrison near San Francisco, one of the toughest in America, the smallest mistake met with brutal punishment, and the men spent their off-duty hours drinking, fighting and gambling.

"It will destroy you," said his father, who knew all about army life, "or drive you insane. Within a year you'll desert, or kill yourself – or someone else!"

Charles had shaken his head and laughed. But it took just three months for his father's prediction to come true.

There was one particular officer who made Charles's life a misery. His name was Captain Smith. He was a short, ruddy, foul-mouthed tyrant, who gained the respect of his new recruits only by selecting one of them as a scapegoat and then persecuting him until he broke. Charles was that man. From dawn to dusk he was bullied and physically punished.

One day, ridiculed and humiliated in the parade ground, he could take it no longer. He fell to his knees and wept.

"Get up!" screamed Captain Smith in fury. "You miserable dog, you gutless, yellow-bellied little snake! *Get up!*"

Too disgusted to waste any more words, he grabbed a rifle and viciously clubbed Charles on the side of the head, sending him sprawling to the ground.

"Sergeant, take this blubbering baby to barracks."

"Yes sir!" shouted the sergeant.

"And in the morning," Captain Smith added, "lock him in the pit."

There was a pause.

"Sir?"

"Are you questioning me?"

"No sir!"

The pit was a bare hole in the ground, covered with a metal sheet. It wasn't wide enough to let a man lie down, or deep enough to let him stand up. Its walls were angled steeply inward, so that it was even impossible to sit down in comfort, and on hot days the heat could be so intense that men had been known to die from it.

Sometime during the night Charles Gratmar disappeared. Sitting in his office at dawn the next day, Captain Smith pretended to be furious, although secretly he was pleased. He had deliberately delayed the punishment so that his victim would have plenty of time to reflect on the pit's many horrors. He had wanted Charles Gratmar to desert, and the pathetic worm had obliged. The punishment for desertion was death.

"Organize search parties," he told the sergeant, "notify all railroads, issue a description to all the sheriffs in the outlying towns. We'll be sure to find him by nightfall."

Left alone in his office, the captain allowed himself a small smile of satisfaction. Then he noticed that there was a letter on his desk. He picked it up and read it.

To Captain Smith

Because I value your death more than my own life, I am going to kill myself. When I die, my avenging spirit will be released. It will stalk your dreams and haunt your mind. Wherever you look, you will see it. Wherever you go, it will follow. Wherever you hide, it will find you. It will never rest until you are dead. It is a pleasure to kill myself.

Charles Gratmar

No one would dispute that Captain Smith was a brave soldier. He had fought well in scores of campaigns, been wounded over a dozen times, and was said to have killed over twenty men. And yet his was merely animal bravery. Just like many bullying, purely physical men, the captain hadn't confronted the darker terrors lurking in the mind. Now, with the letter clutched in his hand, he swallowed nervously. Not that he was going to let a piece of paper disturb him. And yet...

Anxiety descended on him. It wasn't like the anxiety that comes before a battle; a soldier is a bad soldier and a fool if he doesn't feel that. This was something else, and something worse: it was the fear of the unknown.

He heard a faint squeaking noise. Looking up, he saw that the oil lamp was swinging from side to side on its hook. He watched it, and slowly became aware that everything in the room was moving: the table was vibrating, the papers on it were shifting, a paperweight fell off the edge and shattered on the floor. Was this it? The first manifestation of the avenging spirit? After a few seconds the vibrations stopped, leaving an eerie silence in their wake.

Captain Smith forced himself to smile at his foolish superstitions, though he stayed motionless at his desk, quietly bemused by the eerie stillness in the air. After half a minute he heard noises and shouts from outside, and then a corporal came rushing in.

"Explosion sir, big one! They say it was at the artillery range."

Captain Smith got a grip on himself. It wasn't the presence of an avenging spirit he had felt – how could it be anything so ludicrous – it had simply been an explosion.

"All right, corporal. Let's go and investigate."

It had, indeed, been a very big explosion. The crater was at least five yards wide. Charles Gratmar had stolen a large quantity of dynamite from the garrison's arsenal, placed it in the middle of the artillery range, and lit a fuse. There was nothing left of the body except tiny fragments of flesh and bone, that were scattered all over the range.

Captain Smith decided to burn the letter from Gratmar, and he threw himself into army life with renewed gusto. He filled his every waking moment with work. But when he finally went to bed at night, his thoughts always drifted to the horrible threats made in the letter.

As he was tossing and turning one night in his narrow bed, phrases from the letter came into his mind... I value your death more than my life... my avenging spirit... wherever you look, you will see it... The captain sat up suddenly, cursing, furious with himself for being such a lily-livered, cowardly... Then he stared at the window.

Although the curtains were drawn, they didn't quite meet, and in the narrow gap between them he saw... No, surely it was only his imagination getting the better of him. There was really nothing there. He looked down, rubbed his eyes, looked up again, and saw an unblinking eye, a nose, part of an unsmiling mouth. *Wherever you look, you will see it...* The face faded away, leaving the captain cowering under his sheets.

The other officers were quite concerned about the captain. He was becoming unpredictable. He would forget what he had said and what he was told, or give contradictory orders. In fact his conduct became so erratic that General Towner, who was the commanding officer of the entire garrison, asked to see him.

Captain Smith prepared for his interview with General Towner very thoroughly. The army was his life, and the thought of losing it was unbearable. He ordered his boots to be polished until they glinted like steel, and sent his uniform back to the laundry three times until he was satisfied its creases were perfect. Looking in the mirror as he adjusted his cap, he saw in front of him a vision of the perfect army officer.

Though his dreams still swarmed with visions of the dead soldier, the captain had received no more night-time visitations. It was true, he admitted to himself, that the dead man's letter had made him nervous, which had led him to make a few mistakes. Now, however, he felt that the worst was over. Who was to say that the face at the window had been Gratmar's face? And as for the dreams, they would fade in time, and he would regain his old authority. He straightened his cap, checked his pocket watch, and set off.

Just as he reached the general's door, a passing soldier failed to salute him.

"You there," rapped Captain Smith, quite pleased to have the opportunity to exhibit his authority outside the general's quarters.

The soldier paid no attention. Wearing a huge, hooded military cloak, he slouched past in an insolent manner. All the captain's long years of army discipline made him feel outraged by this blatant display of insubordination

"You there – halt!"

The figure stopped.

"How dare you fail to salute an officer!" Captain Smith bellowed, marching up to the man. "Turn around, soldier."

Slowly the figure turned around and lifted its head. Captain Smith saw a pale face with both eyes closed. Then the eyes opened. They were the glinting, accusing eyes of Private Gratmar. The captain's new-found confidence oozed away. He stepped back.

"Leave me alone!" he begged.

Unsmiling, expressionless, the figure slowly shook its head from side to side. Then it raised a long, pale finger, and in an unmistakable gesture, drew it slowly across its throat, like a knife. Its eyes closed, and it turned around and glided away.

"Captain Smith, there you are!" called the general a few seconds later from his open door. "What are you hanging around outside for? Come in at once!"

The general quickly decided that his captain was

mentally ill, and ordered him to take two months' compulsory sick leave.

Captain Smith's condition did not improve at the sanitorium he was sent to in San Francisco. Everything the letter had predicted was coming true. The spirit *did* stalk his dreams and haunt his mind. If he looked out of his window onto the sanitorium's secluded lawns, he sometimes saw the dead man gliding between the trees. If he went into the city, the dead man would be sure to follow him. The captain's health deteriorated even more, and within a few weeks he was fighting for his sanity.

In a last desperate effort to get better, he decided to visit a medium. There were many of these in San Francisco. Nearly all of them were unscrupulous cheats. They claimed they could communicate with the dead, and charged money for making up the stories that their clients wanted to hear. But by now the captain was so desperate that he was prepared to try anything.

"Well now," said the medium, an old woman with long, white hair, "I know you have suffered a great deal recently."

"Yes I have," Captain Smith whispered hoarsely.

"You've done the right thing, coming to me," she said, thinking she could easily charge an army captain double her usual fee. "Let me place my hands on your head... Now, tell me the nature of your suffering."

In a hesitant, stumbling voice, he recounted how he was being haunted by the spirit of a dead man.

"He is a man I treated badly," he whispered, "a man I drove to take his own life! Now he comes before me, in a hooded cloak, and opens accusing eyes that bore into my guilty soul!"

"Yes, it's true!" the old lady hissed, "I can sense it, you bear the guilt of his death!"

The captain moaned.

"Don't despair," she continued. "There is still time. I must call up the spirit of the dead man."

"Can you do that?" came the quavering reply. "Will he come?"

"In the spirit world, my dear, nothing is certain, but, if the powers are with us..."

"I don't want to see him!" Captain Smith sobbed.

"Don't worry," said the medium in a soothing voice. "He will most probably be visible only to me." Inwardly she was relieved that her client didn't want to see any ghosts himself. Some people did, and could be quite awkward when they didn't appear.

"Now, what was his name?"

"Gratmar – Charles Gratmar."

"Close your eyes, and try to concentrate on his spirit if you can."

The captain did as he was told. Her hands moved down his head, over his shoulders and arms, to take hold of his own hands. Swaying from side to side, she started to make a strange groaning noise.

"Charles Gratmar!" she called at last, "Charles Gratmar! You who have passed to the other side, reveal yourself to us, the living!"

As she churned out the same old words that she used on every deluded fool who came through her door, Captain Smith whimpered.

"Aaah..." she sighed, "he is appearing, I can see him..."

"You can?"

"A soldier, in a big cloak!"

"Yes!"

"Who opens *accusing eyes!*" the medium hissed.

"Yes!"

"He has been greatly wronged. He cannot rest until the living and the dead have made their peace. Charles Gratmar, will you, who have departed this first world, now acknowledge the regret and guilt of the one who wronged you? Will you cease to afflict his tortured soul?"

"What is he doing?" Captain Smith pleaded, opening his eyes to stare at her, "What is he saying?"

"He is bowed down under the grief of his own death," she answered, gazing as though at something far away. "He puts his fingers to his temples. There are tears in his ghostly eyes. Charles Gratmar!" she called once more, "you who walk with the shadows of the dead in the unknown lands, release this man from your curse! Release him!"

She started to shake violently. She was preparing herself for a big finale, when the spirit of Charles Gratmar would miraculously smile in reconciliation and goodwill, and she could announce that the curse had been lifted and Captain Smith forgiven. She opened her eyes in blissful readiness for this superb proclamation, then screeched in stark, raving panic and stumbled backward, pointing at the doorway.

Standing there, ominous and unmoving, in a dark cloak with an overhanging hood, was the spirit of Charles Gratmar.

"Holy mother of Jesus, save me!" the old lady whimpered.

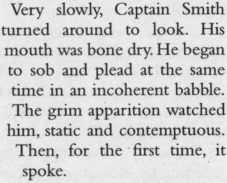

Very slowly, Captain Smith turned around to look. His mouth was bone dry. He began to sob and plead at the same time in an incoherent babble. The grim apparition watched him, static and contemptuous. Then, for the first time, it spoke.

"Tonight," it whispered in a rasping monotone, "you will die."

"No-oooo-ooooo!" cried the wretched captain.

"Wherever you have looked, you have seen me. Wherever you have gone, I have followed. Tonight, wherever you hide, I will find you."

The captain put his hands over his eyes, shaking in terror and grief. The next time he looked, he was alone with the old woman.

"Get out of my house!" she hissed at him. "You are an evil man. Get out at once, get out!"

Captain Smith stumbled out of the medium's house with only one thing on his mind: escape. Almost running down the street, he found a carriage company and hired a carriage, promising to pay double if he got to the next town by midnight. Within twenty minutes of seeing the hooded spirit, as night descended on the State of California, he had left the city of his torment behind.

It was a cold night. The carriage driver pulled his blanket over his shoulders and urged the horses to go faster. He had concluded that his passenger, who was as strange a man as he had ever met, was probably fleeing from the law. As he contemplated this, he thought he heard something above the clatter of the galloping horses – an odd noise, somewhere between a shriek and a choking sound, like a shrill splutter. He reined in the horses.

"Hello there!" he shouted, leaping down from his seat. "Is everything all right?"

There was no reply. He took one of the lamps from its holder at the front of the hack and walked around to the side.

"Hello there!" he repeated, knocking on the door. Still there was no reply.

As he held up the lamp his eye was caught by something glistening on the side of the carriage. He touched it, then examined the dark circle of liquid at the tip of his finger – blood! It was streaming from the gap at the bottom of the door and dripping onto the ground.

Before opening the door, he hesitated for a few seconds, looking around him as though help might miraculously appear from somewhere. He knew he had to do it, so finally he took a deep breath, grasped the handle, and pulled – then sprang back with a cry of disgust.

Captain Smith's body must have been propped up against the door inside. The top half flopped backward out of the carriage. The head lolled from the blood-drenched neck and fell against the side of the carriage with a dull thud. It hung there, upside-down, pathetic, the throat slit from ear to ear. The man was as dead as a doornail.

For some seconds the driver's eyes locked onto the grisly sight, before he raised his lamp and looked into the dark interior of the carriage. He was convinced that there was some murderous evil lurking within. All he could see inside were the lifeless legs of Captain Smith, and yet he wailed in terror.

"Mercy! Don't kill me! Please!"

From beyond the other side of the carriage, behind the dust-stained window, was an unflinching face. It peered at the driver from within a sinister hood. Something in its deathly stare petrified him, leaving him rooted to the spot. Then it moved away into the darkness.

One day, many years after these events, an elderly man arrived in San Francisco. He had been brought up in the city, but it was forty years since he was last there, and he gazed in wonder at the new buildings and the trams. He was an expatriate American, returned from a life of wandering in Europe, who had decided to spend the last years of his life in the city of his youth.

Over the next few weeks he explored all the places he had known, saving until last the garrison, where he had served as a young soldier. Instead of the rough collection of wooden cabins he recalled, it was now a sophisticated military academy. A courteous private was assigned to show him around and answer all his questions.

"This building here is the new laundry, sir. It has a steam press that cleans a hundred uniforms an hour."

"A hundred uniforms an hour, you say."

"Yes sir. And if you look over in that direction you'll see the..."

"Do you like the army, boy?"

"Yes sir, I guess I do."

"Ever been bullied?"

"No sir."

"When this garrison was only a few shacks in the dust, a man could get bullied beyond endurance. In fact the truth is, a man could get bullied to death."

"Were you a soldier here, sir, long ago?"

The old man looked at him.

"I knew someone who was, son. His name was Charles Gratmar. He was bullied, and beaten, and punished, and so badly abused and humiliated that he couldn't take it no more. And so he planned a revenge." The old man breathed in deeply and watched a platoon being drilled with flawless precision across the parade ground. "A terrible revenge. An *original* revenge."

Slowly, watching the eyes of the young soldier register first boredom, then interest, and finally repulsion, the man told the story of Charles Gratmar's suicide note, and of the explosion in the artillery range.

"That's one way to go," the private observed. "There must have been little pieces everywhere."

"Everywhere," the old man agreed, nodding thoughtfully, "*and yet Charles Gratmar was still alive.*"

The private stared at him.

"You see son, Gratmar didn't attach himself to that dynamite. He used a hog."

"He er, erm... A hog? Why?"

"Don't you see? He faked his own death."

His listener was now utterly captivated. The man explained how Charles Gratmar started to "haunt" the captain, until Captain Smith became so deranged that he was forced to take sick leave. He described how, finally, the "spirit" spoke to its broken victim for the very first time.

"What did it say?"

"It told him he would die that night. It drew its finger across its throat."

The private whistled.

"Captain Smith fled, but Charles Gratmar

followed him. Know what happened?"

The private shook his head.

"Gratmar got into the carriage the man was fleeing in. Captain Smith broke down, like the lily-livered worm that he was. He begged, and sobbed. Gratmar just watched him, took out a razor blade, and turned it over in his hand."

"What happened?"

"Gratmar slowly reached across, until the blade was inches from the cowering man's neck. 'Take it!', he hissed, and the captain, who was in his power, grasped the razor with a trembling hand. For a long while Gratmar's glare bored into the terrified eyes of the man who was seconds away death. Then..."

"Then what, sir?" whispered the young soldier.

"Then the spirit of Private Gratmar ordered Captain Smith to do something."

"What did it say?"

"It said: 'Slit your throat, and meet your doom.' "

"Smith slit his own throat?"

"By this time he was grateful to slit his own throat."

The young man looked at the old man with a sense of wonder and repulsion, observing the faint smile that played around the corners of his mouth.

"It was *you*," the soldier breathed.

One Silver Bullet

It was three o'clock in the morning and the city of London was as quiet as a church. Alex Collier was patrolling the area near Liverpool Street Station, keeping an eye open for break-ins. His hobnailed boots rang out sharply on the cobblestones, echoing in the clear night air.

Alex was a nightwatchman. He worked from midnight until six in the morning, seven days a week, and he had done so for eleven years. It was usually a quiet job. There were times when he encountered troublesome drunks, and there was the odd burglary to deal with, but in all his years as a nightwatchman he'd only been in serious danger three times.

He looked up. Rapid footsteps were approaching from somewhere. A man suddenly hurtled into the street from a side alley, running at him full pelt.

"Help me!" he panted, grabbing hold of Alex's arm and looking back over his shoulder in panic. "It almost got me, near London Wall, and the noise it made!"

"Calm down!" Alex ordered. "Calm down and tell me exactly what happened."

"I... it..."

The man was too terrified to explain properly. Without any warning he bolted.

"Hey you, come back!" Alex shouted, but in seconds the man had vanished down another alley.

Alex made his way to the street known as London Wall and walked up and down it. He was puzzled by what had happened and by the man's strange words: "it nearly got me". What did he mean by *it*?

"I suppose I'll never know," Alex muttered. Then he heard it.

Imagine a noise so appalling that it stops you dead in your tracks. It was similar to the noise of a wolf baying at the moon, a sound which has struck dread into the human heart for thousands of years; but it was worse than that, far worse. It was the noise of everything that is horrible, a howl of evil, dying out slowly, lingering in the air like a foul stench.

Alex breathed out tensely, and his heart started to pound. Never, in his whole life, had he been more certain of anything: no human being could have made a noise like that.

The following night he forced himself to patrol London Wall several times. He didn't hear that horrible noise again. Nor did he hear it the next night, or the one after that. He started to think about it less and less, and within a month he had put the incident out of his mind altogether.

Alex liked a hot drink before he started work, and there was a street vendor with a stall near Liverpool Street Station who sold tea and roast chestnuts.

"I'm cold through and through," said the old man one night, pouring tea into Alex's battered tin mug. "I want to get to my bed."

"It's the best place to be on a night like this," Alex said with a smile.

"It is, sir. Good night to you."

"Good night."

Alex had seen this vendor nearly every night of every week for years, and was familiar with all his habits: the way he leaned over his roasting chestnuts to keep warm, and the way he muttered to himself as he methodically counted out his earnings. He seemed as permanent as Nelson's Column in Trafalgar Square. Yet, before the sun rose, the old man would be dead.

An hour and a half after buying a cup of tea from the street vendor, Alex was in his local police station.

"I was expecting a quiet night," he said. "Criminals like a dark night or a good thick fog, but there was a full moon."

The sergeant conducting the interview nodded.

"I was about halfway through my rounds when I walked past the entrance to an alley off Ellis Street. I peered into it, then went on my way, but..."

"Yes sir?"

"There was something odd, which I couldn't quite put my finger on. I went back to the entrance of the alley. I still couldn't see anything, but I realized what was so odd. There was an unmistakeable smell."

"A smell of what?"

"Of roast chestnuts. I walked down the alley and I came across his cart. It was smashed to pieces, and there were chestnuts everywhere." Alex looked up at the sergeant. "Well, you know what I found next."

"Tell me in your own words, sir, if you would."

"The alley leads into a cobbled yard. Even before I reached him I knew he was dead. It was the angle of his neck. And then I fell."

He sighed heavily, and put his head in his hands. "I was a few yards away from him and I tripped over something, and I found myself on my hands and knees in a pool of sticky liquid – blood. I'd tripped over his leg. It had been severed clean off."

Alex put the evening paper down, stared at it, and picked it up again. He was in a state of shock.

MURDER IN THE CITY

EXPERTS MYSTIFIED BY HORRIFIC WOUNDS

The body of a man torn limb from limb was found in the city early this morning by Mr. Alex Collier, a nightwatchman. The badly mutilated remains of Mr. Eric Baxter, a seventy-year-old street vendor, were discovered in a back alley. It is believed that one of his limbs had been severed. Police are refusing to speculate publicly about how the victim met his death, but it is known that experts from London Zoo have been asked to examine the body. The possibility that an unknown wild animal is loose in London cannot be discounted.

"What could it be?" he asked himself. "What could it *be?*"

His wife, Jane, stood next to his chair, watching him anxiously.

"Go to bed, Alex. Get some rest."

"He was alive. At midnight he was alive, and then a few hours later..."

"Alex..."

"I never thought I'd see anything as horrible as that. You'd never think that a human being could be altered into that pathetic mess of torn flesh."

Jane began to cry. Her shoulders shook, and the tears streamed down her face.

"I'm scared," she said.

"Oh Jane, I'm sorry, but I can't get it out of my mind. You don't need to be scared."

"I'm not scared for *me*," she gulped.

For the next few days the newspapers were full of wild animal stories. Some speculated feverishly about escaped circus lions, while others pursued a story that a well-known aristocrat had released three pet tigers into Hyde Park because they had become too big to handle. People were advised to stay in after dark, or to travel to their destination in a carriage, and mothers were told to keep their children's bedroom windows closed at all times. But there were no further attacks in the succeeding days, and the press eventually lost interest. Within a month the issue was all but forgotten by everyone except Alex and the police.

"Alex," Jane said one night, just as her husband was tying his bootlaces.

"Yes?"

"I don't think you should go to work tonight."

"What?"

"I don't think you should go to work tonight."

He looked at her with an expression of surprise and confusion on his face.

"Why not? You know I never miss a night."

"What if that... *wild animal* is out there again?"

"But it's been four weeks since it struck! If it is a wild animal, that is. I'm starting to think all that talk about animals was nonsense. Anyway, I've worked every night since then, so why should tonight be any different?"

"I don't know, it's just that..."

"What?"

"I don't know," she said, sighing heavily. "I just don't want you to go out there tonight."

"Well, I've got to. How are we supposed to live without money?"

With that he stood up, kissed her, picked up his lamp and left.

It was a full moon again, but Alex didn't notice. Striding along the city streets, he was preoccupied with thoughts about Jane. He was concerned about her health. She was usually very cheerful, but in the last few months she had begun to seem almost melancholy. She looked pale and dispirited, and she was sleeping badly. Alex sighed sadly, and wondered if he could persuade her to go to the doctor.

Ahead of him, a figure in a bowler hat was hurrying none too steadily along the street. It was

probably a drunken young city gent going home after a night out on the town. The man got to the end of Leadenhall Street and then turned right into Bishopsgate.

Suddenly, there was a loud, piercing scream. It lasted only a few seconds. It was followed by an equally sudden, ominous silence. Alex started to run towards it as fast as he could. Wondering what he was going to find, he turned the corner at full speed and skidded to a halt. The man in the bowler hat was alone and unharmed. He was standing stock still, staring down at something in the road.

Alex walked up to him slowly, stood beside him and looked down. There was something in the gutter. It was the smashed body of a beggar boy. He was lying on his back, with his hands pressed against his ribs, almost as if he were trying to hold his chest together. Perhaps he was; a great slash had torn his body open from the neck to the navel. There was an expression of petrified astonishment on his face.

The young man next to Alex stepped back and sat down on the pavement with his head in his hands. Alex blew three shrill blasts on his whistle to alert the police, then looked up and down the street – and saw it. About fifty yards away, crouched in front of a wall, was the most gruesome and evil creature imaginable, a creature half human and half animal, standing on two legs but with a body covered in hair, and with the snarling head of a wolf.

"Look!" Alex shouted, turning around to grab the young man, "look!"

The young man, however, seemed to be in shock, and didn't respond. By the time Alex turned back to the creature again, it had gone.

A policeman came pounding into Bishopgate, slowing down as he saw the body. He almost tiptoed up to it, then put his hand to his face.

"Another one!" he said. "There's a savage animal on the loose, that's for sure."

"I've seen it!" Alex exclaimed. "Just now, I looked up, and it was over there by that wall!"

"What was it, sir? A big cat of some sort. A tiger?"

"It was a..."

"Sir?"

"It was a werewolf."

Back at home, Jane watched Alex with concern. He sat with his fists clenched tightly, a look of frustration on his face.

"Jane, I'm telling you I saw a werewolf with my own eyes! I'm not imagining it. It was the most gruesome thing I've ever clapped eyes on. I went to the police station to make a statement, but when I told them about the werewolf, they sent me home, warning me not to waste their time. What will happen if I can't get them to believe me?"

"Try to see it from their point of view," Jane argued. "Most people think that werewolves are a myth that was created centuries ago to scare people.

Why should they believe you saw something that, in their eyes, simply doesn't exist?"

"I don't care how unlikely it seems. I know, because I was there. *I saw it*, and I don't doubt what I saw. Are you saying that you don't believe me either?"

He looked at her, and his eyes flashed with anger. She met his gaze.

"Jane? Do you believe me?"

Then, slowly, she turned away from him, wanting to conceal the anxious tears that were beginning to fill her eyes.

"I believe you," she said.

Once again the people of the city talked in hushed, frightened tones about the savage bloodlust of the creature prowling around London, while the newspapers were full of sensational reports and wild theories. But even the wildest theories didn't go so far as to suggest that there was a supernatural being out there. The only people who thought that were Alex and Jane.

Because he couldn't get the police to listen to him, Alex started to research the subject of werewolves on his own. Every afternoon he would go to public libraries to hunt down books on supernatural subjects: witchcraft, black magic, vampirism. It was in a battered old volume called *Devils, Demons and the Forces of Evil* that he finally found what he was looking for:

WEREWOLVES

These creatures were once the innocents of God, whom Satan has corrupted. Truly, though they bear the outward aspect of men and women, yet they are demons. At the rising of the full moon their evil is manifested, for then they can no more prevent themselves from turning into monstrous beasts than the Earth can stop turning.

Some become wolves. Others become half man and half wolf. A werewolf has the strength of five men, and must drink blood or die. It stalks lonely places, hunting the solitary pilgrim or lost child. It kills quickly, and drinks deep.

Werewolves can conceal their foul hearts under a handsome countenance, living unsuspected among their fellow men. Yet wherever there are many unsolved killings, it is certain that a werewolf is loose.

These agents of the devil must be killed by stabbing thrice in the forehead, or by shooting once through the heart with a silver bullet. A werewolf may seem dead when killed by other means, yet whether buried or burned, on the night of the next full moon it will return.

A werewolf betrays itself when injured, for then it returns to human form. An injured werewolf always seeks darkness and sanctuary wherein it may conceal its foul secret. It must not be allowed to escape, but must be followed and killed, for it is the duty of all who fear God to thwart evil.

Alex read that page again and again. He just couldn't imagine himself confronting a werewolf with a gun and a dagger. He was just a nightwatchman, not a hero. And yet, if he didn't do it... who knew what might happen? He snapped the book shut and strode out of the library.

He found it relatively easy to get hold of a dagger and a gun, but finding a silver bullet proved to be next to impossible. All the gunsmiths he contacted had never heard of bullets made of silver. Antique dealers claimed never to have seen one. In the end, Alex commissioned one from an old silversmith, a tiny man with a deeply wrinkled face, whose hands were as delicate as a child's.

"A bullet?" said the silversmith dubiously, after Alex explained what he needed. "You want a bullet made of silver?"

"That's right."

"But what on earth would anyone want with a silver bullet?"

"You don't need to know why I want it."

"If you want to shoot someone, use an ordinary bullet. It's far cheaper."

"Will you make me a silver bullet or not?" Alex snapped, impatiently.

Carefully considering this question, the old man smoothed his leather apron under his hands.

"You only want one?"

"One is all I need."

"It'll cost you a guinea," the silversmith warned.

"Very well. I'll give you twelve shillings now as a deposit," Alex told him, "and the rest when you've made the bullet. It has to be ready before Friday, do you understand?"

"I'll do my best, but..."

"If you can't do it before Friday then I'll go somewhere else."

The man shrugged and nodded.

Friday was the night of the next full moon.

"Alex, what are you *doing?*" Jane asked, as he put his gun into his jacket pocket. The dagger was already in his belt. "You'll lose your job if you're caught carrying a gun."

"You know what I'm doing," Alex replied impatiently, "because I explained it to you. And it's better to risk being caught with a gun by the police than be caught by a werewolf without one."

"But why should *you* have to face it?" Jane asked, wringing her hands. "One man against that thing... if you meet it you won't stand a chance! Stay here, Alex. If it really does exist the police will find out eventually. Let them deal with it."

"And how many more people will have died in the meantime?"

"Alex, don't go!"

It was too late. Her husband stamped out of the room and left the house. He was determined not to let Jane's anxiety deflect him from his task. Jane sat down on a chair, clasped her hands together, and began to pray that he would be safe, and that the werewolf wouldn't materialize. But an icy fear gripped her heart.

Alex made his way down past the Old Bailey to Blackfriars Bridge. At the riverside he stopped. He was slightly out of breath. Although there was nothing out of the ordinary to be seen or heard, Alex somehow knew that he and the werewolf were fated to meet one another that night. He decided to make his way westward, through the back streets to Covent Garden.

A few minutes later, passing under an iron railway bridge, he jumped in alarm as a train rumbled overhead. The sound it made was deafening. The whole structure of the bridge shook, and although Alex pressed his hands against his ears, he couldn't block out the noise. It went on and on as each carriage thundered past. It seemed to get louder, too – so much louder that it hurt to hear it, causing Alex to cry out in alarm.

Only when the bridge stopped shaking, yet a nightmarish howl continued, did he realize, with dread, what had happened. The roar of the werewolf had merged with the noise of the train. It was a roar, not so much of fury, but of torment.

As the howl faded out, Alex slowly took his hands away from his ears. Suddenly even the silence was threatening. He patted his hip to check that the dagger was still secure in his waistband, then, cautiously withdrawing the gun from his jacket pocket, he advanced.

From under the railway bridge he emerged into a narrow alley. To his right was a dark, windowless warehouse; to his left, a series of low brick arches set into a high wall. He tiptoed forward. As he came level with the opening of each arch, he pointed his gun inside: the slightest movement and he would...

"Aah!" he shrieked.

Alex had been determined to try to kill the werewolf as soon as he got half a chance, but when it advanced from one of the arches, and he saw it close up for the first time, his body failed to obey his mind. He dropped the pistol.

It was hideous to look at, with its huge, wolf-like head, and its evil eyes surrounded by furrows of furred skin. Fresh blood stained its teeth and spattered its fur. The monster didn't attack. It watched. Alex was only a few yards away from it. He could hear its curious rasping breath, see its heart beating under the matted fur of its chest. But it was looking into the creature's eyes that appalled Alex. It was as if he were looking into bottomless pits of evil.

Quickly he bent down to pick up his gun, but before his fingers could close around it the werewolf attacked him. It leaped across the cobblestones faster than a striking cobra and dealt a ferocious blow that sent him spinning back. He crashed into a wall, feeling his own warm blood begin to seep from the torn flesh of his face; the werewolf's claws had ripped into his cheek.

Alex knew that, without the gun, his only chance was to stab the beast in the forehead three times. However, against such savage power, the task did not seem to be possible. Even so, he closed his hand around the handle of the dagger. The monster stopped in front of him, then it threw its head back to howl at the moon.

No one could act while such a horrific noise split the air, and all Alex could do was try to endure it. At last it stopped. As Alex cowered against the wall, the beast lowered its head to stare at him. Its mouth suddenly opened and then snapped shut, making its heavy jowls ripple. Saliva dripped from its jaws.

It was on him in a moment, snarling and snapping,

knocking him to the ground and pinning him down with its claws. Alex coughed and spluttered at the rank smell of the creature's breath. He screamed in agony when he felt its mouth fasten onto his shoulder. The dagger was still in his hand. It was not possible to move his arm, but his wrist was free, and he managed to jab the weapon upward.

The surprise of the pain, rather than the severity of the attack, made the werewolf spring back with a roar. A slight wound on its thigh started to bleed. Alex got to his feet and advanced with the dagger. He slashed and hacked, determined that if he was going to die he would at least die fighting. More by luck than design, a wild slash with the razor-sharp dagger connected with the werewolf's arm.

The werewolf roared in agony, and held up the stump of its left arm. At its feet a bloody hand closed and opened, quivering as though still alive. The werewolf roared again and delivered another lunging blow that sent Alex sprawling to the ground. Then it fled, holding its wounded left arm in its right hand.

When Alex came to a few minutes later, he groaned. The back of his head throbbed where it had struck the ground, and there were cuts and and rips all over his body from the teeth and claws of the creature. He staggered to his feet and picked up the pistol that was lying a few yards away. A trail of blood leading in the direction of the river indicated which way the creature had gone. He set off in pursuit, but returned almost at once to retrieve the severed hand; if he failed to find and kill the werewolf, at least the hand would provide evidence of its existence.

He soon found himself going down a set of slimy wooden steps that led to the bare mud of the riverbank, an ugly place that stank of sewage and dead fish. At first he couldn't make out the trail of blood on the dark mud. As he looked up and down, not sure which way to go, the severed hand twitched in his grip, and he dropped it with a little yelp of fear. Looking down, he saw that it was changing! The claws were receding and becoming nails, the hair was becoming shorter and vanishing... of course! He remembered what he had read in the library. A wounded werewolf seeks darkness and sanctuary, and changes back into its human form!

He crouched down to watch, fascinated, and saw it transform into something utterly different from the murderous thing it had been; the skin was now pale and smooth, the fingers long and delicate. He was looking at a woman's hand with a gold wedding ring on the wedding finger.

Alex sank his face into his hands and let out a cry of animal despair. Farther along the river, a woman started to sob. It was Jane.

"Alex!" she shrieked. "Alex!"

He staggered along the bank and found her. Where her left hand should have been there was a bleeding stump, which she clutched in agony. She looked so pathetic and weak, nothing like the evil demon she had been a few minutes before.

"Oh Jane!" he cried, not knowing if she was a murderer or a monster, or the woman that he loved. "Why?"

"I've been cursed!" she sobbed. "I can't help it! Forgive me!"

"But how did it happen?" he cried.

"I'm not sure," she whimpered. "I don't, I can't — some time ago I had a dream, a terrible dream. I saw wolves running in packs under a huge new moon, chasing a man, while a great beast laughed and howled! The next morning I felt ill, but I was all right the day after. I was fine, until..."

"Until what?"

"Until the next full moon."

"How... how long has it been going on?" he asked, utterly appalled.

"For six months. Alex, you must believe me, it's not me who does those dreadful things. Do you think *I* could try to kill you? It's the werewolf, it takes me over. After each time," she whispered weakly, still clutching her injured arm, "I tell myself I'll never kill again, that I won't *let* my body change, but when the full moon comes there's nothing I can do to stop it!"

For a few minutes they could do nothing but cry.

"Alex," she said finally through her tears, "if I could have killed myself I would, but a werewolf can't destroy itself. You know there's only one way to stop these murders from happening."

"What do you mean?"

"You know what I mean!" she suddenly shrieked. "Kill me, Alex, I beg you, kill me!"

He started to cry again, sinking down next to her in the mud. The great city slept, and the river flowed slowly past, as it had always done. Alex held her in his arms, tighter and tighter.

"Isn't there any other way?" Alex whispered to her.

"No. You must be strong, Alex. Do it. Do it now!"

A few seconds, later a single shot rang out across the dark surface of the river.

The Head of Jean Cabet

One spring evening in the middle of the eighteenth century, near a small village in the province of Beaugency, in France, a group of villagers stood around a pond. There was barely a breath of wind. High above, skylarks sang. It should have been a beautiful and tranquil scene. It wasn't. Out in the middle of the pond, a body was floating, face-down in the water. A dagger had been plunged into the middle of its back.

The villagers were silent. The only noise was that of the birdsong, until the sound of galloping horses made the villagers look up. Three horsemen were racing across the fields, kicking up soil and mud behind them.

"Make way for the law!" one of them shouted, a soldier, leaping from his horse and pushing villagers out of his way. A second soldier was helping Martin Desalleux, the elegantly robed Public Prosecutor of Beaugency, to dismount. It wasn't usual for such a high-ranking official to investigate the scene of a crime, but Monsieur Desalleux had been in the area visiting some of his officials when news of the murder came in.

He was a handsome man in his mid-thirties. He had pale blue eyes, jet-black hair, and an air of such authority that the simple villagers, watching him as he glanced at the body, shuffled nervously. Gradually, even the chattering stopped, leaving an eery silence.

"Fish it out," he ordered the soldiers.

They waded into the water and hauled the body up the shallow bank.

"Turn it over."

The body was flipped onto its back. When they saw the face, most of the villagers let out shocked gasps of recognition. An old woman shrieked and sank to her knees by the corpse.

"Pierre! Pierre!"

It was her son.

"Who is this man?" he asked her, but she was too shocked to reply.

"Come on," M. Desalleux said sharply, addressing the group, "I haven't got all day. You there, what was his name?"

"Pierre Leroux, sir."

"What was he?"

"A farmhand."

"Anyone know why he's been murdered?"

There was no response.

M. Desalleux sighed, staring in exasperation at these dirty, sullen people. Frankly, he didn't care if illiterate peasants murdered one another, as long as there were enough of them left to do all the work, and he certainly wasn't going to waste much time on the incident. On the other hand, it was the solemn duty of the law to identify a murderer and bring him to justice.

"What's your name?" he asked one of the villagers standing nearby.

The man stepped back a couple of paces, looking puzzled. He was perhaps twenty years old, with a mop of tousled brown hair hanging over his frank, handsome face.

"My name?"

"Yes, *your name.* What is it?"

"Jean Cabet, sir."

"What are you?"

"A farmhand, sir."

"You're a farmhand too, are you? Well, Jean Cabet, I'm placing you under arrest on suspicion of the murder of Pierre Leroux."

As the villagers looked at him in amazement, a young woman pushed her way to the front of them, screaming, "No, no! Please sir, it wasn't Jean!"

"*Me* sir?" Jean Cabet said. "But I don't understand, I never... I don't... I haven't..."

"You will be taken without delay to the town of

Orléans, where you will be held until the date of your trial."

"Sir!" the man pleaded, sinking to his knees, "as God's my witness, I promise that I've never laid a finger on Pierre! I would never do such a thing. What evidence do you have?"

"I daresay I'll think of some."

"Leave him alone!" the young woman wailed.

"Hush, Marie," Jean Cabet said, afraid that she too would be caught up in the nightmare that was unfolding before him.

"Are you the suspect's wife?" the Public Prosecutor asked her.

"We're engaged to be married, sir."

Martin inclined his head in mock courtesy.

"Congratulations," he said.

"Thank you sir," the young woman whispered, beginning to hope that this powerful man might change his mind.

"But I think we can safely say that the wedding's off," he added.

The soldiers suddenly grabbed hold of Jean. Marie let out a scream.

"Please don't take him!" she wailed piteously. "He's innocent, I swear!"

But within minutes the man she loved had been tied up and taken away.

Six weeks later, a jeering crowd lined the streets near the gates of the prison in Orléans. They were waiting for the "notorious murderer", Jean Cabet, to be taken to the Place du Martroie, where he would be executed. Six weeks had given the rabble of the city plenty of opportunity to discuss Jean's case. His notoriety had grown. He was said to be a thief, a spy and a highwayman, as well as a murderer, and in the past two years alone was said to have killed more than twenty people.

At his trial the judge, having considered the evidence presented by Monsieur Martin Desalleux, had described Jean Cabet as "one of the most dangerous and notorious villains ever to have passed through these courts". Jean had been sentenced to death by beheading.

The gates of Orléans prison opened, and soldiers on horseback rode out in front of the open cart that carried Jean Cabet. The crowd surged forward roaring "Murderer! Murderer!" and soldiers on the ground had to beat it back.

"Filthy killer!"

"Scum, scum!"

"Die, murderer!"

The journey to the Place du Martroie took nearly an hour. Jean was untied and then dragged from the cart to a wooden platform. When he saw the man who was standing there, he shuddered; it was his executioner, the man who was going to end his life. He was a huge figure concealed under a black hood, who leaned nonchalantly on his axe. The crowd, in a frenzy of bloodlust, bayed for the execution to start.

Once Jean had been hauled onto the platform he was given the opportunity to talk to a priest.

"Before God judges you, do you confess to this murderous crime?" the priest asked. "Do you repent?"

"But father, I'm innocent."

"My son, remember that these are your final moments on this earth. This is your last chance to save your soul from eternal torment. Do you repent?"

"I have nothing to repent," Jean answered quietly.

"Then you must prepare for hell," the priest said.

Jean looked into the crowd, and there, among the rowdy, jeering thousands, was the grief-stricken face of his beloved Marie. He hadn't seen her since that terrible day when he had been arrested. She was standing motionless, holding a handkerchief to her tear-stained cheek. There was a brief moment for them to stare at each other helplessly before soldiers grabbed Jean and dragged him over to the block. He was forced to kneel in front of it so that his head hung over the edge. To his left he could just see the executioner's feet. They were clad in highly polished, black leather boots, and next to them was the head of the razor-sharp axe, which was going to...

"I'm innocent, and God knows I'm innocent!" Jean called, to the delight of the watching crowd, which heartlessly burst out laughing.

The executioner walked up and down the platform, weighing the axe in his hand. He took a stance behind Jean, and slowly lowered the blade of the weapon until it was just touching the nape of the condemned man's neck. The crowd fell silent. Only then, in the stillness of those last few moments, with the edge of an axe poised over his neck, did Jean truly understand that he was going to die.

"God save me," he whispered.

The executioner raised the axe high above his head. Sunlight glinted on the metal of the blade. The silence was absolute. Not a man, woman or child moved a muscle. Then Jean sensed the executioner move, and in the last half-second of his life he heard the axe rushing down, the faint whistling noise that it made in the air, the...

Fifty yards away, M. Desalleux watched the proceedings unfold, seated in the stand that was specially erected for the wealthy on such occasions, He saw the ignorant head of an ignorant peasant bounce on the platform – once, twice – before rolling to the side and coming to a rest on its right cheek. The eyes were wide open in astonishment, the mouth was contorted with shock, and blood was streaming from the severed neck.

M. Desalleux winced. It was a gruesome business, but the important thing was that a case of murder had been dealt with quickly. He firmly believed that the swift and brutal enforcement of the law helped to deter crime in general; sometimes, he convinced himself, the innocent had to suffer for the benefit of everyone else.

Six months passed before the Public Prosecutor had to deal with another murder. A woman had been robbed and stabbed on the outskirts of the city, and there was no trace of her attacker. However M. Desalleux authorized the arrest of a vagrant – any vagrant. He wasn't going to let a sentimental attachment to justice get in the way of an efficient legal process.

As he worked at his paper-strewn desk the next day, fabricating the evidence that would convict the unfortunate vagrant, Martin Desalleux couldn't help but feel very satisfied with himself. His work was easy and lucrative, and his reputation was growing. The only thing he felt he lacked was a wife.

He leaned back in his chair to stare out of the window at the evening sky. His views on marriage were as straightforward as his views on the law: he didn't care if his future wife loved him or not, as long as she was exceptionally wealthy. Smiling at the idea of suddenly being rich merely by marrying someone, his thoughts couldn't have been further away from Jean Cabet. Nothing could have prepared him for what happened next. He turned back to his work, dipped his pen in the inkwell, and started to write — and it was then that a heavy object fell from nowhere onto his desk.

Martin Desalleux let out an instinctive shout of surprise, which changed almost immediately into crazed shrieking when he realized what he was looking at: it was the head of Jean Cabet.

It bounced on the desk — once, twice — before rolling to the side and coming to a rest on its right cheek. Its eyes were wide open in astonishment, the mouth was contorted with shock, and blood was streaming from the severed neck... onto his papers. As M. Desalleux, white and shaking, gripped the arms of his chair so hard that one of them broke off, the accusing eyes of Jean Cabet stared deep into his own.

"Good afternoon, Monsieur Desalleux."

M. Desalleux panted in terror at the deep, mocking tone of its voice. To see it there, lying on its side, *talking*... it was unbearable.

"*You!*" he breathed. "Why aren't you... you should be *dead*."

"No, Monsieur Desalleux," came the ominous reply; "*you* should be dead."

M. Desalleux whimpered and sobbed. He was so

terrified that his body was unable to withstand it, and he fainted. He slumped forward, and his head struck the desk and rested, face down, on the desktop. He was still unconscious when his manservant entered the room in the morning. But the head had gone.

It took M. Desalleux a long time to recover. The doctor who examined him declared that he had suffered from an acute and spontaneous attack of bleeding from one of his ears, and he refused to believe his patient's trembling account of how a severed head had dropped from above.

"You must try to accept that what you saw was an illusion brought on by the severity of your condition," the doctor told him.

"But I saw it with my own eyes," M. Desalleux whispered feebly.

"No, you *think* you saw it with your own eyes. A sudden loss of blood can lead to all sorts of strange hallucinations. Believe me, I've dealt with dozens of similar cases."

"But..."

"Anyway," hissed the doctor, leaning down to whisper in his ear, "do you really want people to think you're insane? Think of your career, your brilliant future!"

Martin Desalleux knew that what he had seen was real, but because it was impossible to convince the doctor, he didn't try to tell anyone else. He confided in no one. But it was difficult to stop thinking about that falling head and what it signified. For months he suffered nightmares in which the head of Jean Cabet dropped out of the sky when he was out riding, or rolled down the street in front of him wherever he walked. He began to realize that the head was haunting him for a reason. He came to the gradual conclusion that he was guilty of terrible crimes.

Martin Desalleux wasn't an inherently evil person. He had once been an honest man, but the power and riches that went with his office had gradually corrupted him, until, by degrees, he had become contemptuous of the rights of ordinary people. He had committed evil acts not because they gave him pleasure, but because it was convenient. Now he properly understood that his actions had been wrong.

Once he had accepted his own guilt, he found that the nightmares became less frequent. When he took up his duties as Public Prosecutor again, his colleagues were amazed at his new-found sense of justice. No one was prosecuted for a crime he hadn't committed, and suspects were often set free because Martin Desalleux considered the evidence against them too slight.

He changed in other ways too. His views about what was important in life altered beyond all recognition. He was no longer interested in wealth or social status. He was a quieter, more likeable man than before. And the final change was that he fell deeply in love.

Michelle was the daughter of a baker. Her mother was dead, and her father earned barely enough money to keep body and soul together. She was a far cry from the woman the old Martin had assumed he would marry, but Michelle was everything that the new Martin could wish for.

They met when her father had been arrested for debt. Debtors were usually put in prison, but in this instance the amount owed was so paltry that Martin had paid it off out of his own pocket. This simple act of kindness had reaped its own reward, because the following day Michelle had come to thank him in person. They had fallen in love at first sight.

They became engaged. Several times before the wedding Martin had tried to tell Michelle — to confess, almost — what sort of man he had once been.

"There's something you ought to know about me," he said gravely on one occasion.

"Is there?" she replied, smiling. "Are you going to tell me all your terrible secrets?"

"Yes," he said, ignoring her light-hearted tone. "And you may feel differently about me once you know about them."

"Rubbish! Nothing could alter my view of you. You're the kindest man I've ever met!"

"Maybe I seem to be now, but in the past, Michelle, I'm afraid I was..."

"The past is the past, Martin, we don't need to worry about it. It would be a strange man who had never done anything wrong in his life. Leave the past where it belongs."

"But you don't understand, I..."

"Now not another word! Forget about the past. I want us to concentrate only on the future."

Martin raised the subject many times, but Michelle always refused to listen to him. In the end he gave up trying to tell her.

On the day that Michelle and Martin were married, there was a lavish outdoor feast. After this was over, Michelle retired to the coach house where they were staying the night. She was exhausted. In the morning they had to get up early to catch a coach to Paris.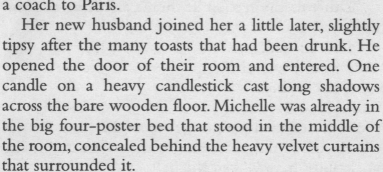

Her new husband joined her a little later, slightly tipsy after the many toasts that had been drunk. He opened the door of their room and entered. One candle on a heavy candlestick cast long shadows across the bare wooden floor. Michelle was already in the big four-poster bed that stood in the middle of the room, concealed behind the heavy velvet curtains that surrounded it.

Martin smiled in happiness. Michelle was his wife! He could hardly believe it had finally happened. She was probably fast asleep, or perhaps she was lying there wide awake, waiting to surprise him and trying not to laugh.

Still smiling, he took off his coat and tiptoed quietly to the side of the bed. From behind the curtain came a long sigh. Michelle was definitely asleep; either that, or she was trying to trick him. Just before he pulled the curtain aside, there was a soft knock at the bedroom door.

"Who could that be?" he whispered, tiptoe-ing back across the room. In the hall a sevant was holding a tray laden with fruit and wine.

"Compliments of the house, M. Desalleux."

Martin tried to suppress his irritation. He'd been through a six-hour feast and it was now nearly midnight. Why would he want anything else to eat?

"That's very kind, thank you."

He took the tray and tried to close the door with his foot.

"Don't mention it, sir. If there's anything else you want, just say."

"I will. Thank you."

"Day or night, sir."

"*Yes.* Thank you."

Finally he managed to get rid of the man. He put the tray down in the corner of the room. Surely the noise must have woken Michelle?

"Michelle?"

There was no answer. It had been an exhausting day, there was no doubt about that. He made his way to the bed. This was the first time he and Michelle had been alone for days. He slowly pulled the curtain back, and the dim light from the candle flickered across the bed. On the side nearest to him Michelle was lying on her left side, her head resting on a long, graceful arm, her shiny hair spread over the pillow. She was asleep, breathing very slowly and gently.

Martin closed the curtain and walked around to the other side of the bed, moving the candle to the little table by its side. He changed into his night clothes. When he was ready, he quietly pulled back the curtain.

Martin tried to scream, but though his mouth opened, no sound came out. On the pillow lay the head of Jean Cabet. It was inches away from

Michelle. Its eyes were closed, and the sheets were drawn up to its chin so that it looked like a grotesque parody of a real man in bed with his wife. Martin could only stare at the repulsive sight. The head's eyes opened and stared back at him.

"Congratulations," it said.

It started to laugh. Michelle woke up immediately and rolled over, her movement pulling the sheets down from the head's chin to expose the severed neck. She shrieked, and it was hard to say which was louder, her terrified scream or the awful, hysterical laughter of the severed head lying next to her.

Martin howled like an animal, insane with fear and rage. He hurled himself at the head, but it rolled away, and its forehead struck Michelle's forehead with a loud crack. Martin grabbed the heavy candlestick and, as the room plunged into darkness, smashed it down, again and again, in a frantic attempt to make the head leave.

It was only a few minutes before the landlord and several other men broke into the room. The candles they carried illuminated a scene that they would always remember, no matter how hard they tried to forget it. They were so appalled that they could do nothing about it, only watch, stupefied.

Martin was dashing his wife's head against the solid mahogany headboard. He looked like a madman. The light from the candles seemed to bring him slowly back to his senses. Michelle's hair slipped from his fingers as he stared up in bewilderment.

Then he looked down at the battered beauty of his dead wife. He gave a cry of grief, and gathered her in his arms, sobbing. She was dead.

Martin Desalleux was beheaded at the Place du Martroie in Orléans nearly a year later. Moments before the executioner's axe descended on his neck, in the instant when every last person in the crowd fell silent out of awe, a sound was heard. The large crowd shuffled uneasily. The executioner, his axe already held high above his head, paused and looked around. It was the noise of laughter, horrible, indescribable laughter, which seemed to come from nowhere and yet everywhere, so that it sounded equally loud to everyone, no matter where they were standing. There was one man there who had heard that laughter before. Seconds later, his head bounced on the platform – once, twice – before rolling to the side and coming to a rest on its right cheek.

More Victorian Horror Stories

Thousands of horror stories were published during the nineteenth century, and some were written by the most famous authors of the time. Many of these have been re-published in new collections and can be found in bookshops, and some are now available as e-texts on the internet. A few recommended authors (and examples of their work) can be found below. The stories range from tales of the supernatural to more explicitly horrific subjects.

Ambrose Bierce (1842-1914): Bierce was an American journalist and author famous for his tales of horror and the supernatural. His work often combines horror and comedy, and is both shocking and entertaining. He wrote hundreds of short stories, including "The Damned Thing" and "My Favorite Murder".

Algernon Blackwood (1869-1951): Though born in Kent, England, Blackwood spent much of his life adventuring in north America and Europe. As well as over 200 short stories and many novels, he wrote children's fiction and poetry. His rich, unsettling style can be sampled in "An Egyptian Hornet". He also wrote a series of stories featuring the "psychic detective" John Silence.

M. R. James (1862–1936): James was the Provost of King's College, Cambridge, and later head of Eton College. He wrote many ghost, horror and fantasy stories, including a novel for children, *The Five Jars*. His imaginative, haunting short stories include "Canon Alberic's Scrapbook" and "The Ash Tree".

H. P. Lovecraft (1890–1937): An American author, he once described his style as "cosmic horror", and many of his stories contain elements of science fiction. One of his most famous – and most shocking – stories is "Herbert West: Reanimator". He also wrote "Supernatural Horror in Literature", a fascinating essay about why people need to read horror stories.

Guy de Maupassant (1850–1893): Though best known for his stylish short stories of French life, Maupassant also wrote a number of horror stories. One of these, "The Hand", is very similar to Mary Cholmondley's "Let Loose" (retold in this book). Other Maupassant horror tales include "Le Horla" – a bleak and frightening work of psychological terror.

Fitz-James O'Brien (1828–1862): O'Brien was born in Limerick, Ireland, and had some success as a writer before emigrating to the USA in 1852. There, his fame as a writer quickly grew and his stories, poems and reviews were published in many magazines. His stories "The Golden Ingot" and "The Diamond Lens" are powerful works of fantasy horror. His tale "What was it?" is retold in this book as "The Beast from Nowhere".

Edgar Allen Poe (1809-1849): An American master of macabre and mysterious tales, Poe wrote several highly atmospheric novels (including *The Fall of the House of Usher*). However, he is probably best remembered for his short stories. Many of these, such as "The Cat" (a different story from the one in this book) are a subtle blend of horror and fantasy.

Mary Wollstonecraft Shelley (1797-1851): Mary Shelley's novel, *Frankenstein, or the Modern Prometheus*, is one of the most famous horror stories of all time. Her other works include the chilling short story, "The Mortal Immortal".

Robert Louis Stevenson (1850-1894): Stevenson's writing ranges from travel memoirs to poetry, though he is probably most famous for his adventure stories *Treasure Island* and *Kidnapped*. His best-known work of horror is *Dr. Jekyll and Mr. Hyde*, which has been turned into many films. Among his shorter works, "The Body Snatcher" is a highly atmospheric horror story.

Bram Stoker (1847–1912): An Irish writer famous for the classic vampire novel *Dracula*, Stoker also wrote many other horror and fantasy tales, including "The Judge's House".

H. G. Wells (1866–1946): Best known for early science fiction works such as *The Time Machine* and *The War of the Worlds*, Wells also wrote horror stories with a supernatural flavour, such as the creepy "Valley of the Spiders".

Another Usborne Classic

VICTORIAN GHOST STORIES

We listened intently. The sound
changed to little pants and fierce sobs,
getting closer and closer, as though a
person in distress were walking to where
we were.

"There's a child out there!" Simson
whispered urgently. "What's a child
doing out so late?"

I remained silent. I knew that it
wasn't a child, not a living one anyway.

Seven spine-tingling stories have been dug up from
the grave and dusted down for this classic selection
of hauntings, howlings and horrors. Enter the world
of ghouls and ghostly apparitions, as the dead return
to torment the living.